Praise for *Thicker Than Blood*

Leary has a deft hand; her clear, intuitive prose offers insight into the disappointments, mystery, and beauty underlying human love.
—Janice Deal, author of *The Decline of Pigeons*

Blind to her adopted daughter's secret struggles with race, class, and identity, a mother confronts the void that is left when a child disappears. Heart-rending from beginning to end, *Thicker Than Blood* exposes the nuances of racism that make it hard for a mother and daughter to connect.
—Marylee MacDonald, author of *Montpelier Tomorrow*

In this elegant first novel, as in the short stories she has published for many years, Jan English Leary proves that she has the eyes, ears, mind, and soul of a dedicated searcher for truths. Her commitment to looking far into each character's side of the story, refusing to take sides, leads not only to deep insights, but to strong and beautiful sentences, which evoke the music of genuine discovery.
—Fred Shafer, editor, writer, lecturer in writing, Northwestern University School of Professional Studies

SKATING ON THE VERTICAL AND OTHER STORIES

Jan English Leary

For Holly & Brendan,
Best to you all,
Jan

FOMITE

BURLINGTON, VT

ISBN-978-1-944388-24-9
Library of Congress Control Number:

Fomite
58 Peru Street
Burlington, VT 05401
www.fomitepress.com

Cover art - © John Leary, *Skating on the Vertical,* detail

For my brother, David English

CONTENTS

EUNUCHS

NATALIE PUT DOWN HER BAG, pulled out her class planner and pens and asked her students to take out their essays on "My Greatest Wish." Earnest but clueless Pak Jeong was the only one to make eye contact, so she called on him to read his essay out loud. He stood, his paper partly covering his smooth, bland face, as he started.

"I very good want the BMW 728. I like the motorcycles." After a few sentences, he lowered the paper and shrugged. The rest of the students glanced at each other and rolled their eyes. Even among those outcasts, themselves strangers to American boarding-school culture, he was a pariah.

"Well, that's a start, but you need to write more than that, okay?"

He looked back at his paper as if there might be more written there.

"Try to write more like you talk. Read it out loud to yourself, and hear how it sounds. That always works."

A few other students read wishes for high-end consumer goods.

"Doesn't anyone wish to *become* something?" Natalie countered. "To learn a skill?"

Blank faces looked back at her, so she asked them to take out their copies of *Night*. However, only two of them had brought their books to class, and she hoped at least some of them had done the reading. Ben Lam had fallen asleep, and Xiao Deng was texting a message from behind his book. When she asked him to put the phone away, he slumped in his chair and shut his eyes.

Getting no response on the reading, she again went over the homonyms *there, their, they're* and the difference between *lie* and *lay*. She called on Xiao to talk about his hero, Yao Ming.

"He's very eunuch."

"Xiao, do you mean unique?"

He nodded.

"First, it's pronounced u-neek, and you can't be very unique. Unique is one of a kind."

They stirred in their seats.

"And you need to know what a eunuch is. Hmm. A eunuch is a person, a man, who has been castrated."

They looked at her, confused.

"It used to be that in some cultures, men would be hired to watch over the harem and they would have their, um, testicles removed."

The boys squirmed, laughing. The only girl, Oh Kyung, lowered her head and stared at her folded hands.

"In China," Xiao said, "that was done very much."

"Okay, so make sure you can pronounce each word correctly. You don't want to say the wrong thing and embarrass yourselves."

On their way out of class, she heard Xiao whisper to Jeong, "Hey, you are a eunuch."

Yes, he could learn. Unfortunately, it was at the expense of the weakest person. She wanted to help Jeong lose the *Lord of the Rings* backpack and the habit of buttoning his shirt up to the top, to bathe more regularly, and, in general, to imitate the students around him more. Unfortunately, he was imitating the wrong things. During study hall one evening, she'd found him behind a row of trees on the edge of campus, lighting a cigarette.

"Jeong? How long have you been smoking? It's so bad for you." How incongruous to see him with his baby face and nerd clothes sucking on a cigarette.

He held up his pack and said, "They are my friends."

She'd been trying to get this group's English language skills up to snuff for the rest of the curriculum at Deighton Hall, but she'd had to scrap her plans for the five-paragraph essay and work instead on basic grammar and vocabulary. It wasn't their fault their parents had, reputedly, paid test-takers to sit in for the entrance exams back home, or that they'd been weeded out from the intellectual elite, the ones who fit the Western stereotype of Asian excellence. She'd come to learn that this remedial course was her test as a first-year teacher, her trial by fire. Succeed with them, and she'd be allowed to stay another year. But she wanted to prove not only that she could do this, but that these weren't throwaway students, seat warmers with rich parents back in Seoul and Hong Kong. They could learn.

And in reality, she found the "better" students more of a challenge, less rewarding. All the grade consciousness without any of the intellectual curiosity. In her junior class that same day, she handed back essays on *Walden*. The one by Topher Adams was suspiciously well-written, as was his last paper. She'd questioned him then about plagiarism, but he'd denied it vehemently and had sicced his advisor on her, who mentioned Topher's wealthy Board-of-Trustees father. This time, she gave him an A-, the minus a craven message that she was on to him. When he took the paper from her, he flipped to the back page, swore under his breath, crumpled the paper, and tossed it into his backpack. For the rest of class, he slouched in his chair and stared out the window, muttering hostile comments and snickering whenever she made a point.

"Topher? Do you have something to say?"

"No." He smirked. "Just listening."

During her first week of classes, Topher had told her this was his favorite class and she naively believed him, thinking she'd already made a connection. Now she realized he'd been playing her for the grade.

Why did she have to waste her time on the entitled in-crowd kids when it was students like Jeong who needed guidance? He was desperately homesick and completely out of his depth at Deighton Hall. If he didn't learn English, he'd told her, and get into an American college, then he had nowhere to go. It was a question of family honor. The minute Natalie gave him the tiniest bit of attention, he started dogging her around campus, showing up at her dorm apartment in the evenings, lamely asking for help on his essays, but since he rarely brought any books, she knew what he really wanted was human contact. His roommate had moved out a week into the trimester, and he was lonely. She wasn't sure if it was a crush or a longing for his mother, but he'd fixated on her. Although she tried to steer him toward his schoolwork, he inevitably drifted toward talk of his family—his elderly father and much-younger mother—and his elaborate family lineage, which he could trace back for centuries. He worried about disappointing his parents, but all he wanted was to go back home to Korea. Natalie recognized his loneliness—after all, she felt like a foreigner herself, a rare Midwesterner among Eastern preppies—but by the end of the day, she was exhausted, her voice hoarse, her eyes red and scratchy. She needed some time to herself. Jeong would linger until she nudged him out, citing his homework and her papers to grade, the truth after all. Then she would lock the dorm, set the alarm, turn out the lights in her apartment, and sit by her window, staring across the courtyard at the hundreds of lights burning in dorm rooms, thinking how she was at once surrounded by people and completely alone. At times like that, she wished she could redo the first week at the school, when she'd foolishly slept with Greg Ryman, a science teacher/wrestling coach, who'd hit on her at the Headmaster's opening cocktail party, urging her to drink another Pomtini and then cradling her arm as she wove unsteadily back to the dorm. Now he ignored her, and she was embarrassed by the knowing smiles the other coaches gave her as she walked past their table in the dining hall.

Clearly, all it had meant to Greg was the conquest of a newbie. That night, after he'd made a dismissive remark about her small breasts, she lay there, pulling the sheet up over her chest as he stepped into his discarded boxers, picked up his khakis, and left without saying goodbye.

She hadn't found any friends yet on the faculty. The women were either faculty wives, preoccupied by their young children, or other female teachers, by and large products of eastern boarding schools like the students. They were all jocks, equally able to trade humor or to give wicked shin-checks, if necessary, with an unkind word or a field hockey stick. Not being a coach, Natalie didn't share that common bond, and none of the English teachers seemed to like talking about books. It wasn't at all like Beloit, where Natalie had had friends and been reasonably happy. Herself the product of public schools, Natalie was convinced that, except for the most challenged inner-city schools, teaching was teaching, kids were kids. But at the boarding school, she found there was a whole lifestyle difference with unwritten rules that the others knew from birth, a kind of innate system of social cues for which she hadn't found the key. The girls in her dorm came for the most part from New York City, Long Island, or New England, and they appeared jaded, wary of anyone not part of their own tight circle. Even though Natalie was barely out of college herself and wasn't a stranger to the easy sexuality of dorm life, these girls seemed disturbingly familiar with HPV, herpes, and casual abortions.

Early on, Lacey Burnett, a senior, had been friendly to Natalie, offering to give her the inside scoop, saying, "This place has a lot of subtext." She started showing up at Natalie's apartment after classes, and Natalie welcomed the break from correcting. It was a good excuse to use her French press coffee maker to make a full pot, which she could never finish on her own. Lacey had arrived at Deighton Hall as a freshman. Her father and grandfather were alumni, so there was never any question that she might not go there as well.

"Next stop, Yale, if I follow the family tradition," she said, winding her thick, blond hair into a coil behind her head. "But it's not a slam dunk like it was in dear old Dad's days."

Lacey asked Natalie what she thought of Greg Ryman. Natalie blushed, wondering if news of her hook-up had leaked to the students.

"I don't really know him," she said, hearing how stilted she sounded.

"He's the teacher 'most likely to.'"

"Most likely to what?"

Lacey laughed and cocked her head to the side. "You know. But

he's a good teacher. You just have to know how to work him."
What did that mean?

Natalie had hoped to be able to advise the girls in her dorm about school work, boys, parents, but it became clear they were more interested in the coffee, soda, and food Natalie offered them than in any kind of relationship of trust. She also dreaded her role of enforcer, knowing that any walk down a corridor could result in discovering weed or alcohol or a boy in a room and then she'd have to report the infraction. This wasn't why she'd become a teacher, but it was a point of honor to prove herself at the school.

Despite her resolve to keep up, piles of uncorrected papers cluttered her desk, and she found she had to value efficiency over careful attention to details. She'd lost an essay from her junior class and was dreading facing the pile until she could locate the missing one.

Although only October, the time had come to turn in provisional grades for the trimester.

Natalie decided to base the marks on what she'd corrected to date and hoped the students wouldn't complain that the grades didn't reflect all their work. She agonized over whether to skew the grades high as encouragement or to keep them low to spur them on to work harder. Her eyes blurry, her head pounding, she stayed up late tallying the scores, typing in the grades, second-guessing herself, re-entering them. That night, she had a dream in which she was standing at a dais in front of a cavernous amphitheater, attempting to give a lecture to students who were yelling, throwing books and pens, wrestling, making out. Because she had laryngitis, her voice came out as a wheeze.

"Hey, you guys! Pay attention! Please!"

When she opened up her notebook, all the semester grades flew off the pages, swirling around the room, and the students trampled them, ripping them to shreds.

At the mid-trimester faculty meeting, Al Sweeter, the Freshman Dean, reviewed the new students' progress. Jeong was mentioned as one of the students risking failure in more than one class, hers being the only exception. When his grades were announced—F, F, D, C-, B+—Natalie heard a snicker from Greg's side of the room. Greg, who was Jeong's dorm master and science teacher, said that Jeong wasn't going to make it.

"The boy is clueless in class and is a lightning rod for hazing."

Natalie raised her hand.

"He seems to me to be a lonely boy who just needs some time to adjust. It's got to be a shock of cultures." She sat back, her pulse throbbing in her throat.

Al Sweeter said, "That's why he's in the Slow Boat to China class."

She looked around the room. Slow Boat to China? Two teachers were nodding.

"Excuse me?"

"We put him in your remedial class because we knew English would be a struggle. If that support isn't allowing him to do the work in his other courses, it's not a good sign."

"But it's only October."

"Time marches on. If he can't cut it, we'll have to flag him."

Greg added that if he weren't such a victim, guys might treat him better. He also said that Jeong owed him several lab reports and if he didn't get them to him in a week, it would be too late to pass the course. Why hadn't Greg alerted Jeong's advisor that he was falling behind?

What a jerk.

When she returned to the dorm after the meeting, she heard raucous laughter and thought she smelled weed. She inched down the hall and traced the smell and noise to Lacey's room. As she arrived outside the door, her hand poised to knock, the voices stopped. She stood there a moment, her heart in her mouth, then she hurried down the hall to her apartment and locked the door.

The following day after breakfast, Natalie ducked into the dark-paneled faculty room, hoping to grab a few minutes alone to correct a set of quizzes before class. She uncapped her pen and fanned the quizzes on her lap, looking for one she knew would be good to start with. Greg walked in, gave her a curt nod, and sat on the opposite side of the room. He took out his *New York Times* and opened it noisily. Distracted by his presence, she tried to work for a couple of minutes, then screwed up her nerve and asked if he could cut Jeong some slack, given how hard it had been for him so far.

Greg said that Jeong was "A day late and a dollar, no, make that a yen, short," then he laughed. When she pointed out that Jeong was Korean, not Japanese, he said, "A joke, Natalie?"

He shook his head.

"Listen. I just want him to be in the right school where he can make it. Better to know that early, so he can find a place to succeed." He glanced over the top of his newspaper and said, "What you don't understand yet is that it's really not fair to all the other students if one drags them down." His eyes darted to her legs, then back to his paper. "You can't save every abandoned puppy you find in the street, Natalie." He checked his watch. "You'll toughen up in time."

"I hope I never get to the point where I'm so jaded I can throw away a person like garbage." And she gathered up her papers, stuffed them into her bag, and rushed out of the room on shaky legs.

After class that day, even though the uncorrected pile beckoned her, Natalie called Jeong over and offered to help him with his lab reports, to get him organized and over the hump. He shrugged.

"This is very important, Jeong."

"I know." He stood there, rocking back and forth on his heels.

"Right after classes today. Come to my apartment. I'll get you out of P.E.. Bring all your notes and your book and we'll straighten this out." He turned to leave. "Jeong, you can do this."

He shuffled out of the room, his slept-on hair sticking up in back like rabbit ears held up by a bully.

That afternoon, he showed up with the plastic still covering his textbook and no notes at all in his spiral notebook decorated with Korean writing. He had no idea what to do for the lab.

"Jeong, you have to help me here. What's the assignment? If you can tell me that, you're on the road to doing it."

"I do not understand Mr. Ryman." His breath was rank, his teeth mossy.

She sat back in her chair. "Did you ever ask him for help?"

"He said, 'Do it like this.' But I do not understand."

She offered to read over the material with him, but he kept straying off topic. He was incensed that students and teachers never got his name right.

"It is Pak Jeong, not Jeong Pak." She told him it was hard for Americans to understand that Koreans put the family name first. "But it is an important name in Korea," he said. "They do not show respect."

"They just don't know. But that doesn't excuse rudeness," she said, handing him a pen.

"Here, let's see if you can write down an opening paragraph."

"My father does not think I work hard."

"He wants you to succeed." She motioned toward the paper. "Where's your dictionary?

Maybe we can look up some of the terms."

"It is fucked." The obscenity took her aback, mostly that he knew the word. He reached in his backpack and brought out a book, which he dropped on the table like a solid block. Someone had carefully glued all the pages together so he couldn't use it.

"Who did this?"

He shrugged. "Some stupid person."

"Jeong, this was a very mean thing to do. I'm so sorry. I'll help you get a new one."

"No one likes me. I want to go home."

"I know, but you have to keep trying. This is the hardest time." She ordered a new dictionary online, and she told him to come again the following day after classes. "It'll get easier the longer you're here." She didn't believe it herself, but she had to pretend it was true.

However, that night, a stomach bug swept through the school, and most of the students, including Jeong, were laid low. She heard that the infirmary had filled to capacity so they were turning students away. At this rate, everyone would be exposed.

Over the course of the next day, one student after another would grab their books and run from the room, while the rest sat there listlessly, heads propped on their hands. By her last class, she asked anyone feeling sick to leave before they got started. Everyone left, even the ones obviously not sick. That night in her apartment, she stared at uncorrected papers, sipping ginger ale and crackers in anticipation of her own nausea, but somehow, she escaped it.

For the next two days, she marked time since no progress could be made with most of the group absent. Because the stakes were low, these were actually pleasant, relaxed classes where she felt a connection with the students. They talked about favorite books and movies and got into a great debate about nature versus nurture. After one class, a student told her it had been the best class of the year, and she reminded herself that this was why she'd become a teacher.

By Friday, the illness had passed, and she planned to take up her sessions with Jeong, worried that he only had the weekend to finish his labs. But he didn't come to class. Natalie called the infirmary to see if he was still there. The nurse said he'd returned to the dorm yesterday. Or the day before, she wasn't sure. No one remembered having seen him in the past few days.

After classes, she climbed the stone steps to the fourth floor of the boys' dorm. As she walked down the hall, competing beats of electronic music and hip hop bled through closed doors. The smells of dirty laundry, body odor, Red Bull, and a lingering tang of weed hung in the air. A student was walking toward her toting a pillowcase stuffed with laundry.

"Where's Jeong's room?" she asked. He pointed to the end of the hall.

When she arrived at Jeong's door, Natalie's heart sank to see that he'd affixed a dry-erase board to the door. Was he expecting friendly messages? Invitations to lunch? Instead, someone had drawn a cartoon of a buck-toothed Asian with an enormous erect penis and pendulous balls.

She smeared the drawing with the side of her hand and knocked. No answer. She knocked again and called his name. Another kid poked his head into the hall and said that Jeong was probably there.

"He's always in his room."

A wave of dread swept through her as she imagined him holed up, having hurt himself.

"Jeong? Are you there?" She put her ear to the door, then tapped it again. "I'm going to open the door. Okay?" She turned the knob. The darkened room smelled like an animal's cage with a desperate, coiled energy trapped inside. "Hello?" Clothes were piled on the floor. One bed was stripped down to a stained mattress. On the other bed, lurking under a tangle of quilts, she detected a curled-up form. "Jeong?"

"Go away. I am sleeping."

She asked him why he hadn't shown up for class. "Are you still sick?"

He said he wasn't.

"Let's get to work on your lab reports then."

"Not now."

"But they have to be finished by Monday."

"I will do it later."

"But, Jeong, Mr. Ryman means business." She waited for a moment and then said, "This is really important. I'd like to help. You can't just give up." She heard the liquid intake of breath, but Jeong said nothing. "Jeong, really. Don't just sit there and let this happen. If you don't do something, it'll be decided for you." She listened to him breathe, and then she shut the door, crossed the quad and dragged herself back up four flights of stairs, the odor of Jeong's room lingering in her nose.

As she walked down the corridor toward her apartment, Lacey walked out of the bathroom, a towel wrapped around her, yelling, "Who the fuck took my tampons? Fuuuck!" She stopped in front of a door and pummeled it. "Rachel! Give me one of your tampons!" She glanced at Natalie. "Hey, do you have any coffee?"

"I can't now. I have work to do." Lacey turned on her heel and walked away. "Sorry. Maybe later?"

Back in her apartment, Natalie tried to correct some papers, but couldn't focus, so she opened her laptop and started a letter to the dean to plead for leniency in Jeong's case. She wanted to state her argument in a few well-formed sentences, but she found her anger spilling out into pages of complaints about the way some students were ostracized, how teachers and the administration looked for ways to exclude those who were different. Anyone, even a teacher who was different, faced blank walls. After writing four pages, she deleted the letter and started again. Each time, the task felt more daunting, the words more muddled. Finally, she put her head down on her arms to take a break.

She woke in the morning with a stiff neck and a headache. Outside her window, she heard a commotion. A group of students had gathered on the sidewalk outside the boys' dorm under a sheet hanging from a top-floor window. She threw on some clothes and ran outside. As she approached the crowd, she saw empty window frames and misshapen lead mullions with shards of broken glass littering the sidewalk. Someone had obviously taken a bat and smashed all the first-floor classroom windows. The sheet had been covered with painted symbols, which she could make out to be a line of Asian writing, done in ink. Her heart sank. You've got to do something, Jeong. She didn't mean that. Half the students were dressed; the rest were in sleep tees and flannel pants. She also saw an agitated Oh Kyung surrounded by a group of students pointing to the sign and talking animatedly. Natalie approached Kyung and placed a hand on her arm. Kyung flinched and looked up. She guided the girl away from the students.

"What does it say, Kyung?"

"I cannot tell you," she said, her eyes welling.

"Kyung. You didn't write it. Just tell me what it says."

She shook her head. "It is not nice."

"That's okay. No one will blame you for this."

Kyung blushed, then said in a very soft voice, "Eat the shit, eunuchs. And the other word is too bad. I do not know it in English."

"That's okay."

Jeong appeared above the banner, his arm raised, fist pumping. He was yelling in Korean, pointing at the crowd and then at the sky. Natalie felt her stomach drop.

A boy behind Natalie whooped then yelled, "Hey, you tell 'em!"

She whipped around to look at a beefy, red-faced jock.

"This is not funny. Have a little decency."

"I didn't do this."

"No. You just make it worse by laughing."

"This kid is hilarious." He cupped his hands around his mouth and yelled, "Hello, dude? We can't read freaky-deaky Korean."

Al Sweeter elbowed his way into the crowd, accompanied by the school psychologist and a maintenance man, pushing a plastic trashcan and a broom. Al and the psychologist put their heads together, looked up at Jeong, then talked some more. Greg joined them, toting a coach's megaphone, nodding as Sweeter gesticulated. Jeong threw a clock radio that landed at their feet and splintered.

"Pak!" Greg yelled. "Stop now before you make it worse." He turned to Sweeter and said that the kid had locked himself in his room. Could maintenance take the door off its hinges?

Jeong appeared at the window, this time with a book. He ripped pages and sent the shredded paper over the crowd, who cheered, "No more school! Revolution!" His face was contorted and red. Natalie could make out occasional English words mixed in with the

Korean—fuck...shit...asshole. More books flew out the window, then his backpack, sailing end over end.

Someone picked it up and twirled it overhead, tossing it to another part of the crowd, and it was bounced from group to group like a raver in a mosh pit. Then he tossed out a lamp and was attempting to lift a chair to the window, but it wouldn't fit through the frame.

"We can't have this," Al Sweeter said to Greg. "He's out of here."

Greg nodded and took off toward the building.

Natalie stood in the middle of these people who'd never given Jeong a moment's notice before now. Jeong was framed in the window, a tiny dictator shouting to his throngs of supporters, who had taken up the chant, "Go, Pak! Go, Pak!" As Natalie watched him face this ugly crowd, however, her dread turned to admiration. As much as she hated to acknowledge it, Greg was right in a way. This was no place for Jeong; he didn't belong here. And this was his way of going home. She wished she had the nerve to make such a spectacular exit herself, denouncing the school for its smug intolerance, the cruel treatment of outsiders. She imagined delivering her screed and then, tossing a sheaf of plagiarized papers into the air to cascade down on the heads of the chastened faculty members, she'd stalk out of the room, triumphant. She studied the bloodthirsty faces around her, turned back to Jeong's window, willing his eyes to meet hers, telepathically sending him encouragement. *Go, Pak. Go, Pak Go, Pak.*

Skin Art

Although Madeline had qualms about traveling to India, a place where brides were burned, poverty was rampant, and corruption ruled, where the water was undrinkable and the food suspect, Bob wanted her to go with him, so she agreed. He'd built a partnership with Indian engineers involving water desalination, and so Madeline saw it as an opportunity to get away with him and relax a bit. After all, she wasn't working at the moment, and they were practically newlyweds; two weeks would be a long time to be apart. Maybe also she'd be distracted from the thoughts of cutting herself that had lately resurfaced after years of lying dormant.

The trip was unbearable—three flights, thirty hours—but she grabbed some sleep in the Frankfurt airport, her head on Bob's lap, legs pulled up fetally, while he stroked her hair and read his notes. When they finally arrived in Goa, she was drunk with fatigue, her joints kinked and stiff, and a spike of pain stabbed behind one eye. Bob's thick hair was mussed, and whiskers peppered his chin, but he still managed to look as if he'd slept soundly. He hit the tarmac at a brisk walk, and she struggled to keep up as they zigzagged around families pushing luggage carts burdened by towers of enormous suitcases. The humid air made her feel as if she were breathing through a mask.

Their driver, a young man named Bhanu, beefy and handsome except for a dead front tooth, held a sign with Bob's last name, WARREN, and tossed their bags into the back of a small van. Madeline had braced herself for the assault of poverty and, once they began driving, she saw beggars lying on curbs, mothers breastfeeding babies, and cows eating garbage thrown in the street.

Bob questioned Bhanu about his childhood, his family, his politics, while Madeline concentrated on not getting carsick as she drifted in and out of sleep in the hot, stuffy vehicle. The air freshener hanging from the mirror coated the air with a gardenia scent that stuck in the back of her throat. Bob wasn't suffering any obvious signs of jet lag. He was jazzed, voluble, as if this were a home to which he was returning. She envied his ability to adapt so quickly to his surroundings.

Leaving behind the city of Panjim and the sea coast with its hotels and crowded beaches, they headed into the country, on roads lined with cashew trees and tall grasses. Bob had rolled up his sleeves, and the open window blew his hair into an unruly bush. Bhanu dropped them off at the lush, quiet resort where Bob had rented a bungalow. Bougainvillea and palm trees lined the paths of stucco bungalows with clay-tiled roofs, shaded by red-flowered vines.

As Bob unlocked the front door, he pointed to the pool.

"See? You can swim and take walks and amuse yourself while I'm off working."

"Yes, it's beautiful, but right now, I have to lie down." She took off her sandals and stretched out on the hard bed for a nap.

"You can't sleep now," Bob said. "You'll never get on the time zone.

You have to resist it," he said. That evening, they were going to the house of his hostess, Saraswati, for dinner with a group of engineers.

"I have to get some sleep," Madeline said.

"Have some tea, and you'll be okay."

"No, Bob. Tea won't do it. I need to sleep."

"Suit yourself," he said, unzipping his suitcase. "But I have to keep going or I'll drop. Trust me."

"Is it absolutely necessary that I go tonight? No one knows me. I won't be missed."

"I want you to be there. And I told them you'd be coming. It would be rude."

"You could say I'm sick."

"I'm not doing that. I'm tired too, but I can't just bag out. This is my work. But take a nap if you have to."

She lay down, but Bob's unpacking distracted her. So she got up, lugged her bag onto the bed, and unzipped it too, hanging up a few of her outfits. Her eyes were dry and scratchy, and a tension knot was forming at the back of her neck.

Maybe if she took a walk, she could shake off her lethargy, but five steps outside the bungalow, the afternoon sun bore down so fiercely that she hurried back inside. Her sleeves stuck to her skin, so she pushed them up, pressing the white, silvered scars on her arms, which faded, then reappeared.

Grabbing her book, she sat by the living room window, nodding off as she tried to read. By then, Bob was happily pecking away on his laptop at the dining room table, wearing shorts and a T-shirt, his hair damp-combed, his glasses replaced by contacts. She knew he was nervous about meeting his colleagues in person and he wouldn't be able to slow down until they'd met.

Madeline was nervous about making conversation with people

she didn't know, particularly when exhausted. She was tired of explaining that her job in advertising had ended through no fault of her own. It just made her sound defensive.

At the airport, Bob had bought a bottle of Feni, a local cashew liqueur, to take to Saraswati and her husband, but Madeline was afraid it might not be what the locals drank, like bringing Minute Maid to Floridians.

She undressed and stepped into the shower, hoping to wash away the layers of grime, but the smells from the trip stayed in her nose—urine and feces, incense, car exhaust, body odor. After a minute, the hot water petered out. The scars on her arms and legs had turned violet under the cold water, like invisible ink appearing on white paper to reveal the message of her secret distress. But no, she told herself, she was done with that.

At six-thirty, she ironed her outfit for the evening, a long black jumper with a blouse, and pulled it on, smoothing the front. The fabric clung to her damp arms. She turned to Bob. "Do I look okay?"

He took her sleeve and tugged it a bit, as if to lengthen. "Yes, you look very nice."

"Do you want to check my arms? Is that what this is all about?"

"Of course not. Come on. Let's have a nice evening. You look great."

"Thanks." Her watch said six-fifty. "Shouldn't we get going? We don't want to keep Bhanu waiting."

"He'll wait for us. He's probably not even here yet." He lowered his palms in a simmer-down motion. "India time. You've gotta slow down here. What's your hurry? You've got nothing to do."

"Thanks, Bob. I needed that reminder."

"Oh, come on. This'll be fun. Remember, don't eat any salad and don't eat with your left hand."

"I know, I know. You already told me. Don't worry; I won't embarrass you."

The sun had dropped in the sky, and the air was starting to cool. They walked, hand in hand, up the path toward the large hand-painted sign for the resort, announcing itself in both English and Hindi. After a couple of minutes, the resort van barreled around the corner and screeched to a halt. Bhanu hopped out, smiling. "Hello, Mr. Bob. Mum."

"Please call me Madeline."

Bob touched her arm and shook his head. They buckled themselves into their seats, and Bhanu accelerated, sending the van bouncing over the dirt road, weaving in and out of lines of cars and around the cows that ambled along, unfazed by the traffic. Madeline was frightened to look straight ahead at what was hurtling toward them, so she focused on the side of the road, the men talking and smoking out front of low huts, the women sweeping the dirt with brooms made of palm fronds, barefoot children scrambling after a soccer ball. At intervals, mixed among the huts, vacation homes for rich Indians and Europeans emerged from welters of weeds.

Bob smiled at Madeline and said, "I'm sure you'll get a second wind. That's how it works with me."

He kissed her hand and she leaned back, closing her eyes to grab a brief nap.

Bhanu pulled up in front of a tall house of dark wood beams connected by whitewashed stucco. They rang the bell, and Saraswati, a short, heavy woman with thick black hair, wearing a green tunic and pants, invited them in. She accepted the Feni with a formal nod, then disappeared into the kitchen. Had they arrived too early?

Inside, photos hung above eye level at a precarious angle,

threatening to pitch them onto the heads of the people below. Saraswati introduced Bob and Madeline to her husband, Vijay, also an engineer, a tall, handsome man with a full gray beard, and their shy, bespectacled teenage son, Samir, who lingered politely before retreating behind a curtain to his room. Vijay's elderly parents were visiting, and after they tottered over to meet the Americans, Madeline offered to help with dinner.

"Oh, no. You are the guest. It has all been arranged," Saraswati said. Behind a curtain, Madeline caught a glimpse of a young Indian woman in a sari and realized, of course, that as a middle-class family, they'd have a regular cook. Madeline was hungry. Bob had said that Saraswati would probably steer clear of dicey food, given that they were foreigners, but Madeline was worried anyway.

Bob launched into an animated conversation with Saraswati about their water treatment project. The older parents seemed to have been invited to take care of Madeline. The mother-in-law was a tiny woman in black slacks and a sleeveless embroidered white shirt. Madeline itched to roll up her sleeves. She stroked her stomach, trying to stifle its loud gurgle. Her legs were wobbly, and she longed to sit down, but everyone else was standing.

The other guests arrived nearly an hour later—Father John Fernandes, a native Goan who was the local priest and teacher at the school, and an ex-pat German couple, Reiner and Anna, and their adopted Indian son, Niko. Reiner engaged Vijay in a discussion of local politics, which Madeline couldn't follow. Saraswati beckoned them to the table and placed Madeline at one corner and Bob down at the other end.

The food looked safe except for the salad, which she avoided. She took dollops of various curries—green, orange, brown—and a piece of puffy bread. Bob was enthusiastically involved in a talk about something called the BJP with Reiner, who had vulpine features and blond hair and managed to incorporate the snobbism of both Europe and Asia.

"Actually, no one who doesn't live in India can possibly understand Rushdie and how he is generally dismissed by Indians."

He never looked at or directed any talk to Madeline. His wife, Anna, was pretty except for a receding chin, a flaw which Madeline found somehow touching.

Madeline's back hurt from sitting on a bench, and the meal dragged on with no sign of ending. To keep herself awake, she studied the photos hung on the dining room wall. Most of them featured stern, sepia-tinted ancestors alternating with portraits of Samir at various ages.

"Have some more food," Saraswati said, passing Madeline a bowl of bright yellow potatoes, sprinkled with fresh parsley. She declined, blushing, then closed her eyes for a moment and felt her head droop forward. It snapped up, and she took a deep breath to revive herself. When Bob glanced her way, she widened her eyes to signal that she wanted to leave. He acted as if he hadn't seen her. She looked at her watch. It was nearly ten.

Her attention wandered to Niko, a boy of about six, with a gorgeous face, bottomless black eyes and spiky hair. He was rolling tiny cars along the floors and striking them with a homemade wooden dagger as he jabbered to himself in German. Madeline ached to run her hand along the velvet skin of his arms, but she knew not to crowd him, so she smiled and nodded.

He grabbed her hand and said, "*Spiel mit mir*," clacked the truck with his sword, then pushed the soft pad of his hand into hers. She looked up to see the adults consumed in conversations, so she leaned over and took a car and ran it around Niko's truck.

When her back grew tired, she lowered herself to the floor. Niko clearly had a scenario in mind, so she pretended to understand and followed his lead. Every few feet, he'd clank his sword on the tiles, yell, "*Halt!*" and give her a menacing look. Madeline reached over and touched his arm.

"Be careful."

As he raised his sword again, the tip grazed her forearm, leaving a long scratch.

"Ow!" She shook her head to caution him.

"Madeline?" Bob asked. The rest of the guests had stopped talking and were staring at her sitting on the floor.

"Niko wanted me to play." Her voice came out tinny and forced, and she covered the stinging scratch with her hand.

Saraswati was frowning, and Bob gave her a disapproving stare. Her face burned, and she lumbered to her feet, sitting on the bench, biting her lip. What do you want from me? she wanted to ask, pressing her fingernails into the meat of her palms to keep from crying.

"Excuse me. Where is your bathroom?" she asked Saraswati, who pointed down the hall. Madeline was relieved to find they had a European toilet instead of a hole in the floor with a bucket of water. She sat and laid her head on the cool porcelain sink to steady herself. When she was finished peeing, she rose and splashed some water on her face. Looking at herself in the mirror, she rubbed some concealer over her eye bags and wished she didn't have to face those people again. To stall, she opened a drawer and found a comb, a stick of incense, and a double-edged razor. The welt on her arm itched to be deepened, to be more than a scratch, a clean cut. She took the blade out, turned it over in her hands, touched the edge to her arm, and then dropped it back into the drawer, her hands trembling.

When she returned to the table, no one seemed to have noted her absence. She wanted to shock them all by letting out a long, anguished scream, but instead, she sat, hands entwined firmly on the table in front of her, heart beating raggedly.

Finally, Bob tapped his watch and gave her a nod, and they thanked Saraswati and Vijay.

"That went great," Bob said, as he placed his hand on the small of Madeline's back and steered her out the door. As soon as they were out of sight, she shoved his hand away.

"What's wrong?" he asked.

"Don't touch me," she said through clenched teeth.

Bhanu was waiting for them out front so she couldn't melt down in front of him. She pinched her arm as hard as she could, fantasizing she was pinching Bob.

When they let themselves into the bungalow, she said, "Don't do that to me again."

"What?"

"You know. When I was sitting on the floor with that boy."

"I don't know what you're talking about."

"Oh, please." A mosquito bit her and she slapped it. Blood met her hand, but part of her welcomed the sting, her pain localized into one sharp pinprick.

Madeline remembered how the X-Acto knife would tickle the skin on her forearms before the thrilling pinch as it broke the surface, drops of blood pearling behind the blade like rubies. It had been year since her last cutting, and the scars were fainter now, but when she ran her hand down the inside of her arm, the edgy numbness made her shiver.

A few weeks after Bob and Madeline started sleeping together, he asked, "Why do you always keep the lights off?" He was her first boyfriend since moving to Chicago, and she was wary of finding someone who would accept her, damaged as she felt.

He pushed, and she pretended it was shyness, but she knew he didn't believe her and might lose patience and leave. So one night, when she burst into tears and he insisted knowing what was wrong, she unfolded her arms and held them out straight. White lines ran across her wrists like scratches on a tabletop.

"They've faded," she said. "I don't do it anymore."

"What are you talking about?"

"Bob, don't kid about this."

He cradled her arms in both of his and ran his hand over the skin gently.

"Those? I can barely see them. What happened?"

She confessed to cutting herself. He listened.

"Promise you won't do that anymore?" he asked, kissing the scars.

She decided that such a man was worth hanging onto. So they were married, and she did fine for a long time, but after the loss of her job, the urge to cut returned. She confided her fear of backsliding, and he gave her a pep talk, but then she noticed that he'd run his hands along her arms, as if to caress them, but he'd linger a moment and steal a peek. Subtle, but enough to let her know he didn't trust her.

Bob was scheduled to spend the bulk of each day in Panjim with local engineers, leaving her alone at the bungalow. At night, he sat up going over his plans while she went to bed. So much for great vacation sex. He was less available than at home. Every morning after he left, she read one of the novels she'd brought until her eyes blurred. She tried to watch TV, but the power was intermittent, and she could only stand to watch so many Bollywood music videos.

At ten o'clock each day, when the cleaning crew came to straighten up the bungalow, she'd follow a path around the pool, through the gardens. At that time of the morning, the guests seeking Ayurvedic treatments would carry their yoga mats back to their bungalows while a lone swimmer did laps. She couldn't muster the energy for swimming or yoga, so she read and waited for Bob to return.

On the morning of the sixth day, Madeline lay in bed as Bob scurried around, dressing for a meeting.

"What are you going to do today?" he asked, as he had every morning so far.

"I don't know," she said, half asleep.

"You should go see some of the sights. Bhanu could take you. That's his job."

"Does it matter to you if I stay here or go out? You'll be busy all day. I can amuse myself."

"Oh, I know that."

She sat up. "And what's that supposed to mean?"

"You know it's not healthy for you to spend all your time alone. Frankly, that worries me." He grabbed his briefcase. "But I can't hold your hand all the time."

"I never asked you to hold my hand."

He shut his eyes and sighed.

"You know, if I really wanted to cut myself, I could do it while you're at work. Without your knowing. But I'm not doing it, okay?"

He stood for a moment, staring at her, then left. When she heard the door shut, she flopped back onto the pillow. But she couldn't fall asleep, so she got up, flipped the switch for hot water, although she knew it was futile to wait, and climbed into a cold shower. Then she put on a dress and heated some water for tea. Her arms were covered with mosquito bites, and she clawed at them, leaving faint white trails of dry skin.

She walked up to the office to check her email. The receptionist stood out front, talking to Bhanu, and it was clear from the tone of their voices and body language that they were flirting. The young woman ducked her head and smiled and readjusted her long, lavender scarf over her shoulder. She was young and voluptuous and she seemed to move on oiled joints. Bhanu leaned against a wooden beam, smiling, not shy about his brown tooth, and Madeline wondered if they were a couple and if they'd been promised to each other by their families.

"Hello, Mum," Bhanu said. She greeted them and asked the receptionist if she could use the computer for the Internet. The young woman wobbled her head from side to side like a metronome. Yes or no? Madeline wasn't sure. Did the woman even understand? Bhanu told her to go ahead, the computer was free, so Madeline walked into the dark office. As she sat behind the monitor waiting for the machine to boot up, her thighs stuck to the chair, and she fanned herself with a paperback. After waiting several minutes to connect, she wrote a letter to her friend Christine, then lost the connection before she could send it. Frustrated, she logged off and trudged back to the bungalow.

She didn't want to eat lunch alone again in the dining room but had not yet managed to introduce herself to the group of German and British visitors.

She swigged a bottle of water and opened a package of cookies. A coat of numbness surrounded her. Teetering on the brink of sleep, she couldn't drop off, nor could she stay awake.

Her book held no interest, and she found herself reading the same lines over and over.

After another shower, she plugged in the adaptor for her hair dryer, and sparks spurted from the outlet, sending a shock up her hand. She dropped the dryer and flopped down on the bed, massaging her tingling fingers. Tears sprang to her eyes, and she pressed the palms of her hands against wet cheeks. Then she stumbled over to Bob's travel pouch and dug through it until she found some nail clippers, the kind with a tiny file. She swiveled the file out and ran the blade along her arm, pressing, waiting for the skin to give way. Just one cut. That's all she'd allow herself. She held her breath and pressed.

"No!" She hurled the clippers across the room, stood up, and paced, kneading her upper arms. Riffling through the pile of resort brochures, she found one for Ayurvedic massages.

A few minutes later, she arrived at the Ayurvedic doctor's office. He took her blood pressure, and she paid him a thousand rupees. Then two young women in saris arrived with twinkling nose rings, each with a jewel glued over the third eye. One of them held a dented metal cup. They walked ahead of Madeline down the stairs, talking and laughing. Madeline wondered if they were making fun of her. They were young, beautiful, dark-skinned, their thick black hair oiled and braided to their waists. Squinting under the hot sun, Madeline watched the braids sway as she followed them along a path and up a stone staircase into a room with a wide-open window. A palm tree fanned the air outside. One of the women handed Madeline a folded piece of muslin with dangling strings and told her, in halting English, to put it on, but Madeline had no idea what to do with it. She'd hoped for a gown—even the paper variety she wore at the gynecologist's—but she stripped naked, glancing nervously at the window, and stood, flat-footed, shrugging as she fumbled with the cloth. The masseuse helped tie it around Madeline like a string bikini bottom, then she put a step next to the table, which was hollowed out like a cutting board. Madeline climbed up and lay in the curve of the wood, then sat up again, crossing her arms over her bare breasts. Calm down, she told herself.

The other woman, whom Madeline figured was the assistant, motioned for her to remove her wedding rings. She hesitated, then slipped them off and dropped them onto a plate. The assistant lit a flame under a tin bowl and poured oil from the cup into the bowl and picked up a cheesecloth-covered bundle of herbs.

"Your skin is bright," said the assistant as she ran her hand along Madeline's arm. She felt herself blush, ashamed of her dry skin, its blue veins and silvery scars.

The masseuse motioned to Madeline to lie down again, and she felt her vertebrae settle into the hard wood. Her belly sank, her hipbones jutting upward.

"Is this the herbal massage?" Madeline asked.

They nodded, again with the metronome head wobble, so Madeline wasn't sure they'd understood. As they stirred the oil, they talked like women sharing confidences. Lifting the bundle of herbs, the masseuse pounded it against the soles of Madeline's feet. She flinched, and the assistant ran her hand along Madeline's arm. After dipping the bundle again, the woman briskly patted it along Madeline's skin while the assistant massaged the oil into her legs and they both rubbed vigorously. Four arms worked in concert, rubbing up and down. Madeline closed her eyes and concentrated on the sensations, pushing out all thoughts except for colors: the blue of the Arabian Sea and the vibrant colors of

Panjim, the oranges and yellows of spices and marigolds from the market.

They rolled her onto her side and arranged her arms and legs, then continued to rub, dip, and pat as she slipped back and forth on the table. The breeze wafted in through the window, cooling the oil on her skin, which now tingled. She felt her joints soften, her muscles loosen, her tension melt away. She worked to slow her breaths, to give in to the rhythm, imagining a phantom lover, a four-handed dark god, juicing her up for a marathon of lovemaking.

A touch on her shoulder signaled the end of the massage. Madeline blinked, surprised to find herself in the massage room. The women helped her sit up. Shaky as a newborn, covered in an afterbirth of oil, she dangled her legs over the side of the table. The masseuse motioned for her to climb down, and she did, on wobbly legs. She peeled off the sodden muslin thong and handed it to the assistant, who threw it on the floor, then took clean towels to wipe her down, a goddess anointed with sacramental oils. Her skin was singing, her Western clothes—pants and a shirt—hung like limp sacks on her new body. The masseuse took a plate containing red powder and ran her finger through it, reaching into Madeline's hair, tracing a straight line along her part.

Madeline bowed, then left the women, floating down the stairs, back to their bungalow, where she fell into bed and slept deeply for two hours.

She awoke tingly with energy, pleased that she'd done something healthy for herself instead of cutting. But she couldn't tell Bob because she didn't want to let on how close she'd come to relapsing. To reward herself, she called Bhanu and asked him to drive her to Panjim. When he picked her up, he handed her a tourist's guide to

Portuguese churches and Hindu temples. "I can show you anything you want, Mum."

"What I really want is to go shopping. Can you take me to some good clothing stores?"

He turned and smiled at her. "As you wish, Mum."

She sat back in her seat and opened the window a crack, letting the breeze blow over her face.

When they reached the business district of Panjim, and traffic slowed to a crawl, Bhanu offered to wait for her, but she told him to go enjoy himself for a couple of hours, that she'd be fine. Pulling the car into a parking space, he pointed out a row of narrow storefronts with gaudy signs and black silhouettes of curvy women.

Madeline wandered into a shop and tried on outfits, finally settling on a salwar kameez, a dark red tunic and pants with a blue scarf. Then she found earrings and a necklace of pounded silver. She stuffed her own pants and blouse into the bag, paid, and went to a restaurant. She ordered tea masala, then sat, watching the people, and soaking up the street scenes. Scooters whizzed by, one driven by an old woman in a sari, another one with a family of four perched precariously on top. Madeline wondered how Bob would react to seeing her out in a strange city, able to get around without him. She finished the strong tea, her head spinning. Across the street, she spotted a sign for mehndi tattoos. Looking at her pale hands and scarred arms, she felt the sudden urge to try something different, to cloak herself in a new skin. Bob would hate it, would tell her she was foolish to sabotage her chances of getting a new job until the dye faded. But he wasn't there, and she wasn't thinking about a job right now.

Madeline entered the shop through a curtain of beads. On the walls hung embroidered cloth with mirrors that caught the light.

An acrid smell filled her nose and made her eyes water. She blinked. A woman approached. Dark brown tattoo swirls laced her fingers and joined in a whorl on the back of her hands. Her liquid black eyes were deeply lined in kohl, and she wore a dark green sari with silver trim.

"May I help you, Mum?"

"I'm thinking of getting one of the temporary tattoos. For my hands?"

"Is this for a wedding?" she asked. A thick line of gray roots ran down the part of her dyed hair, but her skin was smooth and unlined.

Madeline shook her head. The woman took Madeline's arm, rotated it, and ran her hand over the silvery-white lines on the inside of her wrists. Madeline blushed.

"My skin is very sensitive. I scar easily. Will there be a problem with the dye?"

"Nothing more than a slight irritation, and only when the mehndi is still on your hands.

Have you decided which designs you'd like?"

Madeline flipped through books of photos and saw hands joined like wings, feet with heels together, toes pointed out. The twirling vines appealed to her, but maybe a mandala on the back of her hand would be interesting.

"What's this?" She pointed to some squiggles in one of the pictures that she recognized as the kind of writing she'd seen on signs around town.

"That's a name, Alok, hidden in a design. For a bride. If the man can't find his own name in the mehndi, then the woman will control the marriage."

Madeline wondered if Bob's name were too American to fit into the delicate pattern. Still, the idea of gaining some control in her marriage appealed to her. She decided on a mandala in the center of her palm with a series of vines that looked like fresh thyme running up each finger and a scallop at the wrist with dots and squiggles, like lace gloves her great-great grandmother would have worn out in the sun.

"Can this be extended further?" She pointed to the wrist design in the picture, then traced a curvy line down the inside of her arm, over her scars.

The woman examined Madeline's arm, and, head lowered, said, "Whatever you desire, Mum."

"Okay. And can you put the name Bob in there also?"

When she paid and left the shop, her arms rigid at her sides, Bhanu was waiting for her by the car, reading a newspaper and smoking a cigarette. At first, he didn't seem to register who she was. Then he smiled broadly and nodded approvingly.

"Well, Mum, you certainly made good use of your time in Panjim."

"I hope I don't look silly," she said, settling into the back seat of the van. But she knew she looked wonderful.

Back at the bungalow, she found a note from Bob, written in caps: WHERE ARE YOU? I WAITED BUT DECIDED TO GO AHEAD TO THE RESTAURANT.

She hurried to the bathroom and rinsed the paste from her arms. The coffee-colored dye had set, and the tattoos contrasted nicely with her fair skin, like sinuous snakes running up her arms, concealing her scars completely. Striking poses in the mirror, she danced around, weaving her hands like a bejeweled woman in a Bollywood music video.

In the restaurant, Bob sat at a table, studying a sheaf of papers.

She adjusted her tunic, threw the scarf over her shoulder, and floated toward him. When she stopped in front of him, she held her hands up, daring him to discern his name nestled inside the mandalas on her palms. He looked at her, puzzled, then asked, "Madeline, what have you done to yourself?" She smiled.

"That's not permanent, is it? Come on, Madeline. Tell me."

She stood there, her head wobbling from side to side, yes no, yes no, enjoying her husband's confusion.

CELL DIVISION

SHARON WAS DUMPING A SOGGY filter of coffee grounds into the trash when her fifteen-year-old daughter, Tamar, came in, wearing the same oversized sweatshirt and leggings as yesterday, her hair a snarled mass of brown and blond streaks. She was a woman-child with skinny legs, full breasts, braces, and an occupied uterus. Her cheeks bloomed with a blush that reminded Sharon of the inside of a petal. Sharon wanted to give her a spoonful of syrupy red liquid, stroke her forehead and tuck her into bed, keeping her on this side of adulthood a bit longer. But it was too late for that, and besides, Tamar would no longer let her in.

"Has Tony called?" Tamar asked, rummaging in the cupboard, clinking glasses and mugs together loudly. "I was in the bathroom."

"Good morning," said Sharon, determined to be pleasant. "No call yet." She tossed the sponge into the sink and sat down at the table. "How are you feeling?"

Tamar poured herself a mug of coffee. "Totally disgusting. I'll be so glad when it's over, and I feel normal again. I'm so sick of puking all the time." She pulled a cigarette from a pack tucked into her sleeve and lit it.

"What are you doing? Put that out." Don't say anything, she told herself. "I thought you quit."

"I don't smoke that much. And it's the only thing that settles my stomach." She inhaled deeply. "At least I'm only going to be pregnant a few more days."

Sharon could almost sense the fetus's nervous system being dulled by the nicotine—the tainted blood flowing through the placenta to its tiny brain. Though Tamar was intent on having an abortion, Sharon wanted her to know that this was not merely the excising of unwanted tissue, like a wart. It was her baby.

As Tamar tipped the mug of coffee toward her mouth, it dribbled down her front.

"Shit!" Slamming the mug on the counter, she stomped off to her room to change.

Sharon had known for about six months that Tamar was sexually active, not because Tamar had told her, but because she'd found a condom wrapper under Tamar's bed. Rainbo Party assortment: cobalt blue. She'd handed Tamar the wrapper and tried to revive the talk about birth control, which they'd had when Tamar was too young for it to be an issue.

"Mom, I know what I'm doing!" Tamar had said with embarrassed irritation. Then about a month ago, Tamar started spending hours in the bathroom, locking Sharon out, finally emerging, mascara smeared around her eyes, wiping spittle from her chin. She also refused to eat certain things—"The smell of fish makes me want to barf." She slept all day on the weekends. And their shared tampon box didn't empty as quickly as before.

So when Tamar brought her the blue-tinted home pregnancy stick a week ago, Sharon wasn't really shocked. They sprawled on Sharon's big bed, Tamar calling her Mommy, soaking the front of Sharon's nightshirt with tears. Sharon had fought back a pinch of pleasure at being asked into Tamar's life again. After the tears wound down, and it seemed as if Tamar were heading toward sleep, she sat up, shook it off and asked, "When can I get an abortion?"

"Just like that?" Sharon asked, although she knew this was really the only option open to Tamar with high school to finish, then college.

"Yeah, I want to." Tamar turned her gaze to Sharon, who hugged her and made an appointment with a gynecologist for later that week.

Nearly every night since, Sharon had been dreaming of children's limbs and torsos mixed up with the garbage in dumpsters, tossed into the air, sucked down wind tunnels. She woke up crying, remembering her four miscarriages. Each one distinct, each one a surprise. The most frequent dream replayed the third miscarriage, the worst because at nearly three months, this was the baby she was sure would take hold. It happened in the shower. She lay under the stream of hot water as the familiar cramps overtook her, and she hoped that everything would wash down the drain. But the tiny fetus, barely two inches long, curled and pink, caught in the filter, and she had to squat down and untangle it from the hair and soap scum. She was terrified to look but found it like a miniature doll, tiny arms and legs already formed, a strange, but real creature. She and Charlie couldn't bear to let the doctor dispose of the fetus, so they buried it in a box in the back yard, giving it their own private funeral. Although Charlie's grief soon ended, she continued to mourn secretly on the anniversaries of her losses, remembering each baby by the names she'd given them: Taylor, Caitlin, Evan, and Morgan. Even though she had no idea about their sex, she felt they should have names.

Every child she lost cut off a line to future grandchildren, thousands of children from later generations. Was she now crying for them, her own lost babies, or for this new one, which Tamar wanted to lose?

While Tamar was being examined by the doctor, Sharon sat out in the glass and mauve waiting room, flipping through back issues of *Working Mother*, trying not to stare at the baby pictures crowding the bulletin board, photos of sleepy newborns with slits for eyes, stair-step siblings in their once-a-year fancy dresses and suits. This wasn't supposed to be happening now to Tamar. Sharon wished she could take Tamar's place, not just to spare her the pain, but because she wanted a baby to replace the ones she'd lost, to replace Tamar who was no longer a baby and no longer hers.

After the exam, Dr. Tourville invited Sharon into her office. With her gelled burgundy hair and teal blue nail polish, she didn't look old enough to be a doctor, but her diplomas looked solid.

"Tamar is about nine weeks pregnant and in excellent health," said the doctor, leaning against the edge of the desk, her slim skirt sheathing well-toned legs. "She knows all the options open to her, and she wants an abortion. Are you okay with that?" Sharon glanced behind the doctor at the plastic model of a woman's abdomen with removable parts, the limp balloon-shaped uterus, the fava bean ovaries, then at Tamar, who sat slouched in the chair, shredding a tissue in her lap. "Absolutely. This is Tamar's life," Sharon said. But what about mine? she thought, surprising herself.

"Of course. Sometimes, there's conflict in the family of a pregnant minor, and I want to know what we're dealing with." Tamar shot Sharon a look that made her wonder what she'd told the doctor.

"All we've done is talk about this for days," Tamar said, her thumb teasing a hole in her tights.

"We've discussed it," Sharon said. "I think it's really the only thing to do under the circumstances." She making an effort to slow down her speech, to hide her anxiety, to appear calm and measured when she really wanted to shake Tamar.

"I just want to get it out of the way."

"That's not the reason to go ahead with this, Tamar," Sharon said. "It's a serious decision, you know."

"God, Mom. That's so insulting."

"I just want you to be properly aware of what's at stake."

"You just want to guilt me more."

"No, I haven't done that. I've been behind you on this."

"Why don't you let this settle for a few days," the doctor said, "and I'll schedule the abortion for next Friday." She took out a fountain pen and scribbled notes in Tamar's chart. "Call me if you want to talk," she said to Tamar, who thanked her and bounded out of the seat, stepping over Sharon's feet on her way to the door.

Hearing the date for the abortion, Sharon felt a sharp tug at her insides and sat back, focusing out the window on the roofs of the buildings outside, her eye falling on the sign for the Halsted Street Mission: Repent now—It's not too late. Sharon sat for a moment, knowing things weren't as settled as she'd thought, but she said nothing.

They drove home in bumper-to-bumper rush-hour traffic, not talking, but not in silence, because Tamar had turned on a blaring techno radio station and slumped down in her seat. Sharon stifled the desire to turn off the radio and force Tamar to listen. It disturbed her that Tamar was treating this abortion so lightly, that she could just toss away a fetus. Did she even understand what she was doing?

Monday morning, Tamar entered the kitchen wearing an acid-green turtleneck sweater, her face shiny and freshly washed but wan. A musky cloud of perfume floated in around her.

"I had to change clothes. And I threw up again. You'd think there'd be nothing left to puke." Her hair dangled in front of her face, and Sharon itched to brush it back. Tamar opened up the refrigerator. "Where's the ginger ale?"

"In the cupboard. There are saltines too."

"I feel so gross." She sat down at the table across from Sharon, her lips chalky from toothpaste. "Was it always this bad for you?"

"From day one, instant morning sickness. I couldn't even come into the kitchen. The smell of any food made me gag." Sharon grabbed a plate and piled it with crackers. "And with the other ones, I was always sick for a while, then I'd feel fine. That's how I knew I'd miscarried. One morning, I'd wake up feeling great, and it was all over."

Just when Sharon thought Tamar was going to talk about it, she stood up and looked out the window.

"There's Tony. Tell him I'll be right down." She went up to her room to get her backpack as Sharon let in sweet, dull Tony.

"Hi, Mrs. Burns," he said. To Sharon, he was just an overgrown boy, all kneecaps and elbows. The shy tilt of his head made it hard for her to imagine him swept up in the throes of passion and guessed that Tamar controlled the relationship.

"Come in, Tony. Coffee? Tamar will be a short while." A thin line of whiskers ran from ear to ear under his chin like the string from a cowboy hat. Too lazy to shave or not yet skilled with a razor?

"No, thanks. I had a Coke on the way over." As he leaned against the door, he readjusted the backwards baseball cap on his matted-down hair.

"So, you have a history test today, huh?" Sharon asked, motioning to a chair, knowing that Tamar would take longer than planned. She hoped Tamar didn't have to throw up again.

"Yeah." He sat at the breakfast nook, his long legs stretched out, crossing one boat-sized shoe over the other.

Sharon wasn't sure what Tony thought about the baby. She knew he hadn't bolted when he found out, and she admired him for that. Sometimes Sharon blamed him, sometimes Tamar. Mostly she blamed herself and wondered if this were Tamar's way of punishing her for the breakup of her own marriage. "Tony, have you and Tamar talked about Friday?"

"Yeah, I'm ditching school that day to take her."

"Actually, I'm going with her. Do you think it's a good idea for you to go too?"

"She asked me."

"How do you feel about this?"

"It'll be hard to know she has to go through it, I guess."

Is that all? Sharon wondered. There was a lot more to it than that.

"Mom?" Tamar stood in the doorway, hair combed, eyes rimmed with black eyeliner, her jaw set in stone. "What are you talking about?"

"It's okay," Tony said. "I don't mind."

Making a point of avoiding eye contact, Tamar pushed past Sharon to gather up her books and stuffed them into the backpack.

"Let me give you some saltines to eat between classes," Sharon said, jumping up, grabbing a handful of crackers and zipping them into a baggie. Tamar took it sullenly, ducking under Tony's arm as she headed out the door.

Sharon watched them walk down the sloping driveway to his dull brown Volkswagen Rabbit with a repainted yellow door. Tamar's head reached Tony's armpit, so her shorter legs scuffled in platform shoes to keep up with his long strides. She looked up at him, her face bursting into an open grin, happier than she ever seemed at home. Sharon decided not to call Tamar back to get her jacket. She remembered when Tamar had started walking to the bus stop on her own in fifth grade, her back straight with pride in her independence, swiveling her head both ways at each intersection. Sharon had stifled the impulse to follow the bus with her car, to flag it down and retrieve Tamar. Every step in Tamar's independence had come too early for Sharon. This time though, Tamar wasn't the only one in the bus. There was also her grandchild.

Sharon piled the breakfast dishes in the sink and headed off to the Book Nook, where she worked part time. Throughout the day, she wondered how Tamar was feeling. Browsing in the parenting section of the store, she found herself looking at books of babies' names, prenatal advice books, titles on early childhood development. At first, she felt the disappointment of knowing she'd never have this experience again, to nurse, to rock her own baby. Then when she came upon a photo of a baby looking like a miniature fencer, one arm arched over the head while the other thrust out, the umbilical stump purple and bulging, she started imagining Tamar actually giving birth. Why couldn't there really be a baby? Charlie could chip in more so Sharon could quit her low-paying job. Then Tamar could leave the baby with Sharon during the day. A ribbon of excitement fluttered in her stomach at the thought of sharing this child with Tamar.

By the time she climbed into the car to drive home, she'd concocted a scenario with the three of them living together. Sharon pictured herself fixing breakfast for both her children, Tamar grabbing a cup of coffee and a cigarette—she was still trying to quit—on her way to the local college and Hilah, her baby, in her highchair and bib. Sharon would spoon oatmeal into her eager mouth and shave off the dribble. They would linger over breakfast and then clean up, watching *Sesame Street* or *Barney* before heading out to spend the day in the park. Sharon would love to take her there, to swing her and to pull off her little socks so she could dig in the sand with her toes. Hilah would slap her hands on the ropes of the swing and call Sharon "Ma" and Tamar "Ta." Sharon would have all the time in the world for Hilah, more than she'd given Tamar. There'd be no rush. Nowhere else she'd rather be. She could give this to both of them.

After work, Sharon returned home and found Tamar's and Tony's backpacks on the floor of the kitchen and realized they were up in Tamar's room, probably in bed. They had sex all the time now. Why not? With no fear of becoming pregnant, no need for condoms, no reason to carry books around with them to pretend they were studying, Sharon couldn't exactly object to the sex.

Sharon remembered feeling very sexual, when she wasn't nauseated, during her pregnancy with Tamar. Charlie found her larger breasts and rounded belly especially desirable and would lie with his face buried in her middle, crooning to the baby, "Hey there, baby, baby boo." She missed him at moments like this and wondered how he'd react to Tamar's news. Would he object to the abortion? Offer to support the baby? Should she even tell him? Everything in her life felt upside down. Tamar was the adult and she was the child, shut out of the adults' private sensual world.

Tamar and Tony came downstairs and Tamar's expression looked both sheepish and entitled. Tony followed her, in a fuzzy post-coital daze. Sharon offered them a snack and something to drink, crackers and herb tea for Tamar, a Coke and a sandwich for

Tony, and invited him to stay for dinner, although she'd have liked to spend time alone with Tamar.

"Thanks, I've got to get home," he said, giving Tamar a look of intimacy not meant for Sharon to see.

"Call me," said Tamar, and Sharon knew he would. They never let a night pass without talking on the phone. Standing next to his car, Tamar stood on her toes, throwing her arms around Tony's neck, tilting her pelvis into him, and they embraced as if they were going to be separated for months. Back in the kitchen, Tamar grabbed a pan from below the counter and opened the silverware drawer.

Sharon asked, "Are you worried about Friday?"

Tamar frowned at the pan and answered, "A little." She opened a can of soup, dumped it into the pan. "I'm trying not to think about it."

"I just—"

"Mom, please." Sharon noticed she'd written her assignments on her hand in ink, a swirl of brown ink like a Moroccan henna tattoo.

"You know. You don't have to go through with this."

"Oh yeah, sure." Tamar scratched a patch of hives on her cheek and dropped her spoon into the pan. "Shit!" she said and fished it out.

"You do have a choice here, you know." Sharon ran her hand along Tamar's back, and Tamar stiffened a bit. "What does Tony want?" An unfair move, playing the Tony Card, but she figured she might get to Tamar through him. "Have you talked about it, to know how he feels? This involves him too, you know."

Tamar was crying now, her head bent, her fingers raking through stiff hair.

"It's your decision, of course," Sharon said. Tamar looked at her glumly. "But remember. Whatever you do, either way, it's permanent." Sharon secretly hoped for the three-month mark to pass so it would be too late for the abortion. "Here, let me do this." She spooned the soup into two bowls and took them over to the table. Tamar slid into her place and plunked her elbows on the table.

"I guess I'd like more time to think about it," Tamar said. "It's happening too fast for me. I just wish I didn't have to do it quite yet."

"So don't."

Tamar was crying silently, dipping her spoon in the soup, letting it fall back into the bowl. "Part of me wants this baby."

"I know. A baby is a wonderful thing." Sharon held her breath, hoping this moment, turned on its side and spinning around like a coin, would land as she hoped. "I would go into your room and check on you. Seeing you in your crib, I'd think to myself, I did this, I made this incredible little creature." She stroked Tamar's arm and longed to stroke her jaw line, its perfect curve, to touch her cheek, which appeared ripe, almost florid. "Your skin was the softest thing I'd ever felt in my life. And you always smelled wonderful."

"What about the diapers?"

"Yours were sweet."

Tamar snorted.

"No, I swear."

Sharon urged milk and vegetables on Tamar and told her stories of her pregnancy. "The cravings. I couldn't get enough Mexican food." She didn't want to overwhelm her and so kept her pent-up desire in check. Tamar's cheeks were now blotchy, her breathing rough and liquid after her crying jag.

Sharon leaned close to Tamar and whispered, "I'll help you if you want to have the baby."

46

Tamar looked up. "What?" Her eyebrows scrunched together, causing a tiny crease between them.

"You know. So you can have the baby."

"I can't have this baby."

"Why not?"

"Oh, my God. I don't know. It's all coming so fast."

"Maybe that's a sign that you don't want to do anything. Hmm?" She took Tamar's hand. "How do you feel right now?"

"Scared. Confused."

Sharon saw the round scar in the corner of Tamar's left eye and remembered how sick she'd been at four years old with chicken pox, awake one whole night, miserable, scratching herself until she bled. Sharon stayed in Tamar's bed with her, trying to urge her to take Benadryl in ice cream, but Tamar wouldn't. They both fell into a bleary sleep at dawn, Tamar tangled up in the sheets next to her. Sharon wished it were that simple now and went weak with helplessness at the sight of the tiny crater on Tamar's otherwise perfect skin.

Tamar hauled herself up from the table wearily, as if her limbs were waterlogged, and took the phone up to her room to call Tony. When she came down an hour later, her eyes were swollen and puffy, but she was giddy, stumbling over her words.

"Feeling better?"

"Yeah, Tony and I talked." Sharon took that as a good sign. Tamar yawned and said she was going to bed. Sharon hugged her and felt her arms cradle two children instead of one. Tamar loosened the tension of her shoulders and leaned slightly back onto Sharon. Then she kissed Sharon and padded off to bed.

Sharon sat at the kitchen table, finishing a lukewarm cup of coffee and watching her neighbor collect plastic toys off her lawn and toss them into the garage.

Wednesday morning, Sharon went out during her lunch break to a maternity shop near the bookstore. As she flipped through the racks of tunics and jumpers, stretchy tops and overalls, she felt excited, as if her own hormones were pumping. Pulling out a purple velour top, she held it up in front of herself and looked in the mirror, imagining how she'd look, remembering how she gained weight everywhere, even her feet—forty-five pounds. When she handed the top to the lip-ringed salesclerk, the woman smiled, probably assuming this outfit was for her, that she was the mother-to-be instead of the grandmother.

At home, Tamar was seated at the kitchen table, books spread out in front of her, scribbling her math homework.

"Tamar, I bought you something."

"What's this?" Tamar eyed the plastic bag.

"It's a bit early, but I couldn't resist."

Tamar dug out the tunic and dropped it as if she'd been scalded. "Jesus, Mom," she said with a look of disgust. "What are you doing?"

"I thought you should have something to wear for those days when you don't feel like squeezing into your regular clothes."

"So I'm fat?"

"No, I mean later."

Tamar's eyes welled. "I didn't say I was doing this for sure. God." She was rocking, curled up into herself, repeating, "Shit, shit, shit."

"I'm sorry. I only thought—"

"Well, this is *my* decision. You can't force me to have this baby."

"I'm not trying to."

"What's this about then?" Tamar threw the bag across the

room, and it skidded across the counter, landing in the sink. "Did you think I'd actually wear this thing?"

"Tamar..."

She slammed her math book on the table, which shuddered. "Leave me alone. You're always telling me what to do. I can make up my own mind about this."

"I just wanted to be sure this was what you wanted."

"No, you just wanted to make sure I did what *you* wanted. You want a baby so badly, *you* go have one. Don't make me do this for you." She turned and ran from the room, slapping the doorframe as she passed it.

Sharon called to her, "Tamar, come back here." Upstairs, Sharon knocked on Tamar's locked door. "We need to talk."

"Leave me alone."

"You come out here." Sharon pounded on the door. "Tamar!"

Tamar turned on music with a pounding bass, and Sharon's hands absorbed the vibration through the door. She looked up at the corner of the hallway and saw a spider web with several tiny eggs suspended in the filaments, rocking perilously. "All right!" as she shook the doorknob, "That's it. You're grounded!"

The door opened and Tamar stood there, laughing and crying, a fresh sweat smell surrounding her.

"What are you going to do, *ground* me for the next seven months so I have to have this baby? It doesn't work that way." She sniffed. "It's not yours, Mom!"

"Will you turn off that music so we can talk?"

"No!" and she slammed the door. Sharon recoiled as if slapped but didn't knock again. Her head was throbbing so she went into her room to lie down.

On her bed, she closed her eyes for a moment. Opening them,

she saw the piles of clothes on the chair across the room. Grandma's old wicker rocker, a low, rounded-back chair with a cushioned seat. She and Charlie used to make love in it, and the combination of the creaking wicker and the awkward acrobatics made them laugh. Sharon suspected Tamar was conceived in that chair. It was also where she used to nurse Tamar—creak, creak, back and forth. Since Charlie, the neat freak, left, she'd let clothes accumulate there, layer upon layer. From her bedroom window, she looked down on the ragged groin of the elm tree out back which had split apart during a spring blizzard a month ago, tearing loose a twenty-foot branch, narrowly missing the house. It now lay splayed and yellowing in the driveway, blocking the garage. She couldn't saw the limb herself and hadn't found the energy to call someone to help her lug it to the street for pickup.

Tamar had been so easy as a baby. Sharon missed nursing her, spending hours playing with her toes, massaging her chubby legs, feeling Tamar's wet breath on her neck as she burped her. Sharon closed her eyes for a moment, pushing on her lids with her fingers and then letting go, so that the blue blobs turned to red and the paisley swirls grew and receded.

Thursday morning, a sunny, spring-like day, Sharon woke up determined to start the day off right with Tamar. But Tamar said she was sick and couldn't go to school.

"Morning sickness?" asked Sharon.

"I just feel gross," Tamar said thickly.

Sharon tucked her in and brought her a cup of herb tea. "Sleep in and maybe you'll feel better in the afternoon." She didn't mention their argument; they'd discuss it later. Before going to work, she checked on Tamar and found her tangled up in the covers, hair spilling over her face, legs drawn up toward her chest.

She drove to the bookstore, but at nine-thirty she called Tamar twice. No answer. She drove home, worrying that Tamar was too ill to come to the phone or that she was miscarrying in the bathroom. At home, she saw that Tamar's jacket wasn't lying on the hall floor where it had been that morning.

Sharon ran up to Tamar's room and started turning over piles of papers on Tamar's desk, a dumping ground for old school work, not a workspace. What did she expect to find? Fear finding? She noticed Tamar's assignment notebook and flipped through it. Tests and quizzes were circled and underlined in bright colors, phone numbers, notes to friends in class, a note, "remember to buy..." Spermicide? Condoms? Pregnancy test? Starting about two months ago, Tamar circled a day with a discreet red P, then started numbering the days. Eventually, the P was repeated with a question mark. P???!!! And then a countdown. Sharon looked at the last entry in the book, today's date. A test in math, then the whole day crossed out except for an entry—appointment at ten— with a phone number. Sharon plopped down on the bed, steadied her breathing, then reached for the phone, dialing the number.

"Meade Women's Clinic. . . Hello, can I help you? Hello?" Sharon waited a second, finding she was mute, and hung up quietly.

How dare she do this without my knowing? And uttering her most secret thought, Why is she taking this baby from me? She looked across the room and saw that Tamar had tacked up a print of an Egon Schiele woman nude, sitting crossed-legged, in the place of her old Britney Spears poster.

Driving to the clinic, Sharon fell in line behind a Volvo station wagon, which crept along, just below the speed limit. She couldn't pass because of the solid line of oncoming traffic. In the back seat of the Volvo, a toddler without a seat belt was facing backwards, bouncing up and down, staring blankly at Sharon. When there was a break in the flow of cars, she pulled up next to the Volvo and glared into the driver's seat at the woman talking on her cell. Sharon blared her horn and pulled ahead, gesturing as she did to her own seat belt.

"Buckle up your child, you idiot!" she yelled. Taking deep breaths, ticking off each second, she forced herself to pay attention to the road, praying she wasn't too late to reach Tamar.

Sharon nearly missed the unobtrusive clinic, located at the end of a strip mall next to a Wendy's. On the sidewalk across from the clinic, a group of pro-lifers lounged with placards, drinking sodas, waiting out the lull between protests. Sharon pulled into a parking space, two cars away from Tony's car with it yellow door. On the frosted front window of the clinic, a single curved line traced the profile of a woman. This could have been a beauty parlor or a nail salon if she didn't know otherwise. As Sharon rushed through the door to the clinic, breathless, sweating, she heard one of the protesters shout, "Murderer! Butcher!" She turned and nearly said, Don't look at me. I'm trying to stop one.

In the waiting room, the atmosphere was quiet, tomblike, punctuated by muffled conversations between clusters of people—a fat teenaged girl and her mother, a woman attempting to corral two bored toddlers, a woman whispering to a man, his arm around her shoulders. In the corner, Tony slouched in a plastic and chrome chair, his arms folded across his chest, earbuds in place, staring at the wall in front of him. No Tamar. For a brief, insane, heart-swooping second, she thought that Tamar wasn't there, that Tony was waiting for her to arrive, listening to some music to pass the time. He could have been waiting for the bus for all the emotion he was showing. Sharon rushed over to the reception desk, where a young woman was talking on the phone.

"I'm Sharon Burns." The receptionist held up her hand to signal for Sharon to wait. Sharon continued. "My daughter, Tamar, has scheduled an abortion, and I want to make sure I can talk to her privately when she gets here."

The nurse pointed to the sign-up sheet with Tamar's signature and returned to her phone conversation. "Next week then? All right." She hung up. "Mrs. Burns, she's already inside."

"I have to see her."

She stiffened. "Please have a seat. It won't help to upset her right now."

"Well, *I'm* upset, okay? I can't believe the mother of a minor isn't allowed to be with her child at a time like this." She turned and glared at Tony, who'd removed his earbuds and had stood up.

"Mrs. Burns?"

"Tony," she said, spitting out his name, "You stay out of this. This is family business between Tamar and me." The stricken look on his face gave her a perverse pleasure. Good, you feel bad. You were in on this. When the door opened to let a patient out, Sharon slipped in, calling Tamar's name.

"Excuse me," said the nurse, touching her shoulder, but Sharon shrugged her off and entered the long, peach-colored hallway, lined with reproductions of pastel paintings, alternating with doors. At the end of the hall, Tamar appeared wearing a hospital gown, her hair pinned back from her face. She looked pale and fragile, but angry, her upper lip flat against her teeth. "Mom. Sssh." She ducked back into the room and Sharon followed her. "I can't believe you're here." There were no baby pictures in this room, only landscapes, flowers, oceans, sky—cheery, bland scenes. No pictures of humans whatsoever, as if any reminder of human life could add to the guilt a woman might feel, as if these scenes could deny what was happening in front of her.

"I need a minute with my daughter," Sharon said to the nurse, who tried to block her entry to the room.

"Tamar, do you need some help?" asked the nurse. "Should I call Security?"

"No, it's just my mother," she said before Sharon closed the door firmly in the nurse's face. "God, Mom." Tamar hoisted herself up onto the table and pulled her knees to her chest.

"What are you doing here?" Tamar glared at her. "We talked about this."

"Yeah, we talked, but that doesn't mean I agreed with you."

"Don't you realize what you're doing?"

"Do you think I'm stupid?"

"It's forever."

"And a baby isn't?"

"Why didn't you tell me? Why did you change the appointment?"

"Because I knew you'd freak out and act like this." She bit her nails and then shook her hand to remind herself not to. "I can do this legally without your permission."

Sharon leaned forward and stroked Tamar's knee. Tamar shrank from her and turned her face to the wall. "Tamar, you'll always regret this. It won't go away. You'll never get over the guilt. A dead baby. Don't you understand?"

"What do you want from me? I'm sorry I can't give you a baby. I just can't do this. I tried to want this baby, but I don't. I don't know what to do. I'm sorry I messed up." Her nose was stuffed so Sharon gave her the box of tissues, and she grabbed a handful, blowing hard.

Sharon rubbed her back, and this time, Tamar allowed her.

"I'm sorry I disappointed you and got pregnant."

"Tamar, I don't want you to do this for me."

"I screwed up big time."

"I just want you to think about it."

"That's all I've thought about for weeks. Do you think I'm taking this lightly?"

She said this with such fervor that Sharon couldn't doubt her feelings. Tamar was rocking again, and Sharon wondered if she were going to sneak her thumb into her mouth for a furtive suck—a habit until she was eleven. She was wearing an ankle bracelet that had started out as a step-up pearl necklace when she was six. Five pearls like baby teeth perched on her anklebone, her toe nails painted green. Sharon had the overwhelming urge to take her home, to spare her all this pain. But it was too late for that. She rocked Tamar, breathing in the mingled smells of patchouli and sweat, gum and tobacco. Tamar's back was exposed so Sharon crossed the panels of the gown, feeling the bumps of her spine like pearls in that necklace. They rocked for a while, their breathing in sync, without saying anything. Sharon closed her eyes and saw Tamar, years from that moment, surrounded by babies, just not this one.

"Tamar. I shouldn't have pressured you. I'm so sorry."

"You didn't. You're here. I wanted you to be here." The mascara had run, and she wiped her eyes with a tissue. Sharon never saw her anymore without makeup, and noticed that Tamar looked ten again. Tamar dropped a wadded-up tissue and reached for another one. "How's Tony doing?"

"I chewed him out. I was so angry."

"Mom." Tamar's expression hardened. "Don't be mad at him. It's not his fault."

The door opened. "Tamar?" asked the nurse, looking at Sharon warily. "Are you okay?"

"Yes, I'm fine," she said, looking at Sharon. "Mom's going now."

They hugged, and Sharon tore herself away, trying to hide the wave of panic that had seized her, making her want to grab Tamar and run. She forced herself to place one foot in front of the other down the hall. In the waiting room, she avoided looking at the receptionist and walked over to Tony.

"Tony?" He looked ready to ward off a blow. "I'm so sorry. I was rude to you."

"That's okay. I know you're upset. How's Tamar?"

She sat down a couple of seats away from him. "She's fine."

"We know this isn't what you want, Mrs. Burns. I'm really sorry we disappointed you. I feel bad that you'll think I'm some kind of lowlife."

"I'd never think that about you." She reached across and rubbed his jacketed arm. He gave off a smell that was at once woodsy and chemical, a manufactured deodorant scent.

"Will it hurt her much?" he asked.

"No, it's early enough, and they'll numb her up a bit."

They sat with an empty seat between them, willing the time to pass. She stared at the same paragraph, unable to read, scarcely breathing, reliving her own D & Cs. Finally, the nurse came to the door to call Sharon in.

"Would you like to see her?" Sharon asked Tony.

"No, I think it'd be better if you went."

Sharon could suddenly see the man he'd become someday—sober, kind, not deep, but good. She didn't hug him, figuring he wouldn't welcome that. She hurried down the hall to Tamar's room, where she found her lying on her back, arms folded across her chest, knees together and tilted to one side.

"Hi, Sweetie," said Sharon. "How are you?"

"Mom." Her eyes filled with tears.

"How do you feel?"

"I'm a little woozy, but okay." She shifted her bottom. "Ow. I'm sore."

A sympathetic twinge shot through Sharon. Tamar laid her arm across her face, and Sharon knew she was trying not to cry.

"I know. I'm sorry."

She picked up Tamar's clothes, found her underwear and leggings, then helped her up carefully, and Tamar felt as light as air, a balloon, so light she might have floated away without Sharon holding her to the ground.

ESKIMO PIE

MARGARET STOOD UNDER A HOT shower to steam away the fog in her head and patted her thighs, feeling for signs of new fat. She'd binged last night, eating nearly a whole pan of chilaquiles, but at least she hadn't purged. Six months and counting since the last time. A record. Hard, since she'd recently gained five pounds.

Her roommate's boxes were stacked in the corner, ready for Eve to move out and live with her boyfriend. Margaret was happy for Eve, but wondered how she'd do on her own. With Eve around, she felt more normal, less chaotic. She dreaded coming home to an empty apartment. How could she cook for just one person? Maybe she could find a new roommate, but the thought of that process wearied her. Maybe she'd finally meet a man, but that seemed even less likely. Her last relationship ended a year ago, and since then she'd had only a few dreary dates.

As she zipped up her biggest pair of jeans, pulled a tunic over her hips, and squeezed her waist, she prayed to the spirits that her least favorite student, Jessica, would stay home today with one of her many vague illnesses and miss the museum trip.

On the drive to school, Jessica's voice looped around in her head. "Ms. Kroll? Ms. Kroll? Ms. Kroll?"

If only she could just tune her out, ignore her, but Jessica always turned up like a speck of dust in the corner of her eye. An awkward child with a nose too wide at the bridge and dull brown hair, she would never be slender or pretty, never the one sought after, always the one left standing alone when teams were chosen. Watching her, Margaret relived her own painful adolescence and felt guilty that she couldn't muster any affection for this girl. But wasn't this why Margaret wanted to teach middle school, to show girls not to base their sense of self on what other twelve-year-olds think of them?

When Margaret entered the classroom, Jessica ambled up with her permission slip, crumpled and smudged. Hillary and Andrea, the Golden Girls, glided in together followed by Wendy Hirschman, Hillary's mother and parent chaperone, wearing full makeup, sleek boots, and a stretchy, black outfit that revealed every muscle she'd toned at the gym.

"Let me make a call and then put me to work," Wendy said, cradling her cell phone under her razor-sharp jawline.

"You're here to help with crowd control, mostly," said Margaret, feeling like a German Shepherd next to a whippet. Wendy nodded and started talking into her phone, laughing and gesticulating.

Margaret felt more comfortable with students than with their parents. Wendy was one of the legions of Room Moms who stayed at home but had appointment books crammed with activities— tennis, Pilates, lunch, shopping, lectures at the Art Institute, benefit planning meetings. At Open House, Margaret felt like the hired help, floating among the guests at a cocktail party, offering canapés on a tray, wiping up spills.

Wendy flashed bleached teeth at her daughter's friends, enveloping each of them in a hug with an air kiss.

"So, wow, the Field Museum, huh?" she said, and Margaret was sure she detected an eye roll. Wendy appraised one of the girl's outfits. "That is so cute."

Because they only had an hour before the bus arrived, Margaret told her students to spend it taking notes, but they never got down to work. Wendy stood at the back of the room, leafing through books, and Margaret felt she should apologize for wasting her time.

At nine-thirty, Margaret herded everyone onboard the bus, which sat, chugging in the front driveway, and she asked Wendy to sit in the back. The kids raced to find seats, pairing up according to their social ranking, knocking Jessica out of the way in their rush. Finding herself without a seat partner, Jessica asked if she could sit next to Margaret, who shifted her shoulder bag to the floor, making room on the seat next to her. Jessica plunked down so close to Margaret that their thighs touched. Margaret itched to push her away but scooted over instead. She massaged her temples to loosen the knot of tension.

Yesterday in class, she'd publicly chided Jessica for her lack of progress on the Indigenous Americans research paper. After three weeks, Jessica had only written a title—Eskimo Food—and some doodles on her paper.

"You have nothing? Nothing at all?" Margaret had indulged herself in saying, and she didn't reprimand Josh when he stage-whispered "Eskimo Pie" and "blubber" to his friend before snickering. It was too easy to make fun of this girl. Imagine an overweight child choosing food as her topic—how clueless—but she couldn't seem to help herself.

The bus lurched onto Lake Shore Drive, heading south toward the Field Museum. The incessant screech of voices shredded what was left of Margaret's nerves, and she repeated her mantra, stay calm, stay calm, stay calm. Bubble gum smells mingled with pubescent funk made Margaret take shallow breaths. For a few seconds at a time, she stole quick glances at the checklist in her lap. No longer than that or she'd get carsick.

She realized that Jessica had been blathering away next to her.

"I told my mom that I didn't want to go to camp this year, but she's making me go."

Jessica's stomach strained against a tight ribbed sweater.

"Maybe you'll have fun."

"I hate camp!" She fingered an angry pimple on her nose. "They think they're so cool, but it's just boring, and I hate the activities. Well, except crafts. I really, really like crafts."

Margaret imagined that Jessica's mother hid the lanyards and dream catchers that Jessica made for her.

"I just want to stay home and hang out and do stuff and play with my Guinea pig." It figured she'd have a disgusting rodent for a pet. "I used to have three, but my brother's dog ate two of them. He knew the dog would eat them, but he let them out anyway."

"I'm sorry."

"That's okay. It's not your fault."

Bristling, Margaret focused on the back of the driver's neck, crosshatched with wrinkles.

"Listen. You're going to have to let me get these papers in order. We can talk more later."

When the bus pulled to a stop outside the museum, several students jumped up and charged the front row.

Margaret stood and shouted, "Sit down and wait until I've counted you!"

Jessica yanked at her coat, caught under her butt.

"Nobody left since you counted us last time," said Andrea.

Margaret glared at her. "Andrea, I have to count you all. It's part of the job. Do you have your partners?"

Wendy was joking with the kids at the back of the bus, not paying attention.

"Guys! Please," Margaret said, her voice breaking. "Find your partners."

Hillary and Andrea smirked and raised their clasped hands to show they were too old for this check. Wendy laughed and raised her hand too. The rest acted as if they hadn't heard her, jostling, stepping on toes, and elbowing each other to get ahead. Jessica was the last one out. She hopped flat-footed onto the sidewalk.

"Jessica, come on. The group is waiting for you." Of course, they were way ahead of her. "Now," she said. "We've got to catch up." She motioned to Jessica. "Let's go." Margaret started walking with Jessica shuffling along, her coat flapping.

As the students streamed across the street, the wind off the lake whipped by, and two girls shrieked, hugging each other. "Stay together!" Margaret called, her voice thinned in the wind. She jogged toward the group, motioning for Jessica to follow.

In the vestibule, other school groups milled around, and her students blended into the crowd.

She shouted, "Borden School seventh graders!" Her words were lost in the chaos, as if she had laryngitis. "Guys, listen to me. Over here." She was strangely out of breath. Finally, she spotted them in clumps. "Now, we're going to enter together and head straight back on the right to the Northwestern Indian section. Everybody?"

"Can we go see Sue?" asked one boy. How could Native Americans compare with the tyrannosaurus skeleton?

"No. Not today. Listen to me. Everybody drop your lunches in the bin here. I hope they're marked properly." Where was Wendy? She picked up the plastic container provided by the museum.

"I thought we could go to McDonald's," said Charlie.

"No, Charlie. I told you to bring a lunch. Mooch from your friends if you need to." Charlie twisted his mouth into a sneer. His friend, Jason, tossed a bag too hard, and it hit her in the stomach.

"Ow! Jason!"

He ran ahead, oblivious. As she was swallowing back her anger, Wendy strolled up.

"Please keep them together," Margaret asked as she fumbled in her bag for the ticket money.

Her hand brushed against the granola bar she'd tucked in to stave off hunger. She broke off a piece and popped it into her mouth, her tongue searching for a chocolate chip among the woody oats. She sneaked tiny bites, wishing she'd brought another one for later. Drawing the worksheets from her bag, she waved them over the group, and they groaned, disappointed.

"Do we have to work?" asked another boy and Margaret stopped short of justifying herself.

She narrowed her eyes and gave him an evil look. "Stay with your partner and answer these questions. Do *not* leave the exhibit. Understood? This should last about forty-five minutes. Now, follow me."

They headed across the central atrium, past the crowds visiting Sue. Hillary appeared at her side with Andrea in tow.

"If we promise to do the sheets on our own, can we just walk around after we're finished? Do we have to do the Eskimo part?

I saw it about a million times when I was a kid." Her eyes swept toward Andrea, whose head bobbled in agreement.

Margaret wondered if Wendy had given them the idea.

"This time is different. We're here to do some work."

Hillary lowered her eyelids and sighed, "Whatever."

Margaret felt her resolve weakening and wondered if it were too late to turn back. En route, several of the pairs had switched to reflect the pecking order of the class. The cool girls were together and so were the jocks, and the lone couple, Ashley and Ben, walked along side by side, with the affected gravity that comes with a first romance. Margaret made a mental note to check that they didn't slip off to make out in the dark recesses of the exhibit. Jessica clomped along a few steps behind her partner, Grace, a competent, focused girl whose clipboard clutched a thick sheaf of paper and three back-up pens.

"Ms. Kroll? Can we go to the gift shop?" Julia asked.

"Just don't start, okay?" Margaret's head was pounding, her mouth dry. Maybe she could slip downstairs and get a soda while they visited the exhibit. The museum was built like a cathedral with a central nave, vaulted and flooded with light, whereas the side aisles were dark and gave off an ancient smell, as if votive candles were flickering in the corners. Margaret led the group into the dimly lit halls toward the Northwestern Indian exhibit, where the sole lighting came from glassed-in cases. Rising toward the ceiling, stood huge totem poles, figures with grotesque lips and tongues whose widely spaced eyes tilted to focus in two different directions. Inside one glass case, life-sized figures of Kwakiutl women bent over fires, cooking food. In another, a fur-clad Inuit man poised with his harpoon aloft, ready to spear a seal.

"Eskimo means 'eater of raw flesh'," she told a couple of students who gazed at her blandly. "However, they preferred to be called by their tribal names—Kwakiutl, Haida, Bella Bella, Inuit."

In the display case, a plaster model of whale meat lay split open. Margaret gagged, thinking of gristle, sinew, and blubber.

"Ms. Kroll?"

"What?" Margaret pivoted and bumped into Jessica, hovering at her elbow.

"Where do I look?"

"Jessica. Give me some space, please." She eased the girl away. "Just look around. I don't know what more to say to you." She jabbed a finger at a nearby placard as if to say, read this, you moron. "Why aren't you with your partner?"

"She went off with someone else."

"Then join up with them and do what they're doing."

"What kind of notes do you want us to take?"

"Jessica. You can do this on your own."

She placed a hand on Jessica's shoulder and pointed her toward a group of students. Jessica stood there a moment, then clomped over and stood right behind Hillary and Andrea, who shot her looks of annoyance. Jessica smiled, lumpy and dumb, clearly unaware of the snub.

"So," Wendy said, having materialized next to Margaret, "how often do you have to do this kind of thing?"

"I don't have to. I thought it would be good for them to see what they're studying."

"Well, yeah, I guess. If you call papier-mâché real. But it beats being stuck in a classroom all day, every day. I don't know how you do it."

Margaret felt the walls close in on her.

"Would you mind keeping an eye on them while I take the lunches downstairs?"

"No problem."

On her way out, Margaret glanced at Jessica, who was sitting by herself on a bench, doodling on her clipboard.

"Jessica? I expect to see some work done by the time I get back."

Jessica's face registered panic, and Margaret felt a delicious pleasure in ditching her.

Margaret lugged the bin down the stairs to the area reserved for school lunches. Ripping a sheet of lined paper from her notebook, she penciled, "Property of Borden School, Ms. Kroll's class," as if that would keep anyone from stealing lunches. Knowing that all those bags were stuffed with food, she fought the desire to sneak a chip, a cookie, something that wouldn't be missed. To calm her grumbling stomach, she decided to eat half of her own turkey sandwich. She swallowed it without a drink, got the hiccups, and felt around in the bottom of her purse for change. The soda machine was out of Diet Coke, so she bought an ice tea and chugged it, then wolfed down the other half of her sandwich in two bites. She fit a dollar bill into the slot, punched the code for chips, inserted more change, and bought a Milky Way. She took another swig of the tea to wash down the chips, then alternated the chips with the candy bar, licking her fingers after each bite, wiping greasy fingers on her jeans. She stopped to catch her breath, her heart thumping as if she'd run two miles. It wasn't even noon and she'd already blown her diet sky high. Despite an overwhelming urge to roll up in a corner and take a nap, she dragged herself up the stairs, holding onto the railing, her head whirling.

Before her eyes could readjust to the darkness, she saw shadowy figures mill around in front of the lighted cases. Slowly, the figures transformed into students she recognized. Jessica ran up, clutching her notes.

"I found some stuff. Do you want to see?" She pointed to a few sentences, scrawled in pencil.

"That's a good start. Now, keep going." Margaret removed her glasses and wiped them clean on the hem of her tunic.

"How much more do we have to do?" Jessica asked, pushing her bangs out of her face.

Jesus. "How much more of the sheet do you have left to do? It's that simple, Jessica. Just read the signs and *do* the sheet." Jessica looked at her blankly. "Look at number five and read that panel, right there."

Head pounding, she took Jessica's shoulders and nudged her in the direction of the cooking display. Jessica stumbled then caught herself, but Margaret froze and imagined Jessica careening into the display case, shattering the glass and cutting herself to shreds. When Jessica glanced back at her, Margaret looked away, her fingers tingling from adrenaline.

How close she'd come to hurting a student. Blindly, she fumbled for a bench and dropped down, forcing herself to breathe slowly. Calm, calm. Vertigo overtook her as if the floor had dropped away and all of them risked being swept into a giant pit underground. She leaned forward to let the blood whoosh to her head.

"Ms. Kroll?" Margaret looked up at Hillary. "We're done." She thrust her finished worksheet before Margaret's eyes, which slowly focused on words neatly penned in gold ink.

"Good."

Hillary and Andrea exchanged looks of complicity. "I mean, do we still have to stay here? It isn't really fair to make us wait for others if they take longer. We've gotten a lot out of the exhibit, and we'd really like to get a Diet Coke." She shifted her weight from one platform shoe to the other.

"Not yet."

"Yeah, but—"

"If I let you go, then everyone will trickle down there and it'll be chaos." Why was she reasoning with them?

Hillary shot her a how-could-you-be-so-lame glance and, after a tsk of impatience and a deep sigh, she turned on her heel to sit with Andrea near the entrance to the room. They glared at her, the warden, the uptight babysitter, the uncool big sister. As if drawn by magnets, other students began to gather around the popular girls, a tableau of disgruntled poutiness.

Margaret felt the weight of the power shift to that side of the room. Her stomach grumbled, and her scalp prickled. She swiped her hand through her hair and gathered up her bag and papers.

"Okay, guys. Change of plans. Let's eat lunch and then we'll come back and finish."

The students leapt up, happy to be released, and raced ahead of her across the atrium and down the stairs to the lunchroom. It took her a couple of minutes to catch up to them, and by the time she did, they'd discovered and attacked the lunches, chattering as they ate. Jessica sat on the edge of the out-crowd table and picked at her sandwich.

In a couple of minutes, they were done, and Margaret instructed them to throw out their trash as they exited. It was hard for her to resist retrieving uneaten food tossed out—whole apples, half sandwiches, bags of carrot sticks, a cupcake with a bite out of it. As she cleared the rubbish from one table, she popped an Oreo and a couple of potato chips into her mouth.

"Ms. Kroll? Didn't you bring a lunch? That's from the *trash*," Jessica said, her face scrunched up in confusion.

Margaret slipped her tongue around her gums. "No, Jessica. I got these from the vending machine. Why don't you head upstairs?"

Someone tapped her on the shoulder, and Margaret jumped. It was Wendy.

"What's the next order of business?"

Margaret could hardly form words; her brain felt sluggish and numb.

"Please go upstairs and keep an eye on them, and I'll be right there." Dizzy, she leaned against the table for support.

"Wait a second," Wendy said. "You have a smudge of something on your cheek." She pointed a manicured finger at Margaret's face. Margaret grabbed a tissue, wiping off a blob of chocolate.

"Oh, thanks. Ick. Messy me."

Jessica was still seated at a table, staring into space.

"It's time to get back to work, Jessica."

"My stomach hurts."

"Come on, get up. You can tough it out a bit longer."

"But I don't feel good," she whined.

"Jessica! I mean it. You've got to stop acting like a baby." Jessica raised her head, stunned. "I can't hold your hand all the time. I expect you to get right back up there. Now! Go! Get out of here!" Jessica jumped up and ran toward the stairs. Margaret grabbed the cupcake from Jessica's discarded bag and stuffed it in her mouth, swallowing it through a tightened throat.

She checked her wallet—no singles—and emptied her change purse into her palm. Thirty-two cents. Not enough for anything from the machine. She rummaged again in the bin and found a partially eaten bag of Chips Ahoy. As she was swallowing, the hard chunks scraping her throat, a young mother with frizzy red hair, feeding her baby at a nearby table, stared at her.

"I lost my kid's retainer," said Margaret. "It's probably hopeless. What a mess."

The woman smiled ruefully and resumed spooning applesauce into her child's mouth.

Margaret dragged herself back to the group, fighting swells of nausea. She sat, breathing shallowly to keep everything in her stomach, waiting for twelve-thirty so they could leave, so she could give them free-reading time until dismissal. Her vision was hazy, and the Inuit mannequins seemed to sway before her eyes, and she reminded herself they weren't real, that she wasn't viewing them through the fumes of a campfire.

Finally, twelve-thirty arrived.

"Guys, time to wind things up. Everyone. Find your partner and meet over here." They didn't move. "Now!" Startled, they began to assemble.

As she counted them, Grace appeared at her side. "I can't find Jessica," she said, not meeting Margaret's eyes. "I haven't seen her since lunch."

"What? Why didn't you tell me before now?"

"I was working and lost track of her," she said.

The prongs of a headache dug into Margaret's temples. Her mind flashed on the image of Jessica, tied up in the back of a van, whimpering, pissing off her captors, holding out hope that Margaret would arrive any minute to save her.

She called Wendy over. "I'm going to look for Jessica downstairs. Don't leave. I'll be back as soon as I can."

"Oh, my God. This is awful. How could that happen?"

She fast-walked through the atrium, but her side kinked, and she had to stop near the swooping backbone of the dinosaur and bend over, afraid she'd vomit in front of a throng of visitors. Slow down, slow down, she told herself as her feet hammered down the stairs. She stuck her head in the door of the bathroom, called,

"Jessica? Are you in there?" and then headed toward the lunch area.

The crowd had left, and the place was strewn with crumpled wrappers. A gray-haired black man with an appliqued museum shirt and hat was sweeping debris into a pile.

Could Jessica have taken off because of what Margaret had said? Panic washed over her, sweat slicking her back. She stuck her head into the hall, but a massive cramp caused her to double over, and she reached out to steady herself. This food was coming up, no stopping it. She ducked into the bathroom, ran to the last stall, locked herself in, and crouched over the toilet as her lunch rushed out in a torrent.

When the spasms subsided, she laid her head on her folded arms and reached up to wave a hand in front of the electric sensor for the flush. Why did this happen today after all those months? When the water stopped swirling, she heard someone sniffle and blow her nose in an adjoining stall.

"Jessica?"

"Ms. Kroll?"

"Oh, my God, Jessica. Where have you been?" Margaret opened the stall to the dingy bathroom, rinsed her mouth in the sink and popped a mint. "I've been looking all over for you. Why didn't you answer when I called you?"

"I did," she said between sobs, "but you didn't hear me."

"Jessica. I want to see you."

A roll of toilet paper had unfurled itself across the floor. The wastebasket overflowed with paper towels.

"I can't. I have a problem."

"What?"

"It's too embarrassing."

"Come on, Jessica. Give me a break." She pounded on the door. Her head was throbbing, her legs wobbly. "Answer me now or you're going to be in big trouble."

Margaret heard a sigh. On the outside of the stall, someone had scratched, "Mandy C. blows guys for free."

"I got my period."

"That's not a reason to run off without telling me." Margaret forced herself to breathe slowly. "Sorry." She looked at her watch. "Get yourself fixed up and let's get out of here."

"I've never had it before."

"This is your first time?" A vision of herself at thirteen, similarly stranded in the balcony of a movie theater, flooded her mind.

"Remember I told you I had a stomach ache? I went to the bathroom after you got so mad at me."

Margaret's face burned. "I'm sorry. Don't worry. We'll fix you up." But the machine was empty. She grabbed a thick wad of toilet paper and passed it under the stall door. "Here. I've done this myself in a pinch. You'll be fine until you're back to school."

"I got some on my pants."

"Wrap your sweater around your waist. No one will know."

"I think they already do. I saw some boys laughing."

Margaret knew they could have been laughing at her for any number of reasons. "Boys are just stupid sometimes. How does that work?" She ran her hand over the surface of the door. "Almost ready?"

Jessica opened the stall. Her pimple had grown redder since the morning, and Margaret wished she could cover it up for her. Her clothes were rumpled, and she looked like she'd been punched in the stomach. Jessica turned on the tap to wash her hands. "Ms. Kroll? Did you get sick from lunch?"

Margaret studied her a moment. Jessica's moon face showed innocent concern. "Yeah. Something didn't agree with me. I'm fine now though."

"I hate getting sick."

"Yeah, me too."

As they climbed the stairs, Jessica touched Margaret's arm lightly and asked, "Is the class waiting? You won't tell them anything, will you?"

Margaret pictured Hillary and Andrea, if they knew, preparing their humiliation so that it was public and painful.

"No. We don't owe them any explanation."

"I'm sorry you don't feel good. Do you think it's the flu?"

"No. Really. I'm fine."

"Because I have some crackers if you think they'd help."

Margaret blinked back the sting of tears.

"Jessica, that's really sweet, but I don't want anything." Jessica smiled at her, and Margaret patted her on the back. "You'll be okay. Think of this as one of those days."

"Yeah, hmm. I know how those are. You had one too, huh?"

As Margaret and Jessica made their way across the sun-splashed atrium toward the assembled group, Hillary, Andrea, and the others stared intently at Jessica, eyeing her for vulnerabilities, waiting so that they could savor her public dressing-down. Margaret admired Jessica for facing them without flinching. For an instant, she entertained the fantasy of spiriting Jessica away so she wouldn't have to deal with the group, to a place where neither of them would have to see those students again, maybe into their own hidden corner of the museum, quiet and dark, sealed off and safe, where they could perform their simple daily tasks, freezing in place only when the rare school group arrived to study the habits of indigenous peoples.

LaTendra

LaTendra's back hurt, and the baby's foot kept kicking a rib, but she had to fix dinner for Terrell and Kaiesha. Mama had started working nights at the nursing home, so that left LaTendra to babysit her little brother and sister. Since she'd dumped Jabarri's sorry ass when he wouldn't claim this baby, she didn't have a boyfriend, and now, with her belly so big, she didn't have the energy anyway. She poured a stream of oil into the boiling water and dumped in a box of spaghetti. While Kaiesha would be happy, Terrell would pitch a fit since he only liked sugar. But that's all he was going to get.

Terrell stood behind LaTendra, tugging on her sweat pants, whining for a cookie, so she stuck her leg out to keep him away, balancing on her other foot. She wanted to get dinner over so she could put him to bed and stretch out herself.

"Kaiesha, come get your brother."

"In a minute."

LaTendra could hear the Power Rangers song and knew Kaiesha was dancing in front of the TV.

"Kaiesha, come on."

LaTendra's feet had gotten too puffy for shoes so she could

only wear flipflops. The baby (she was sure it was a girl) sat low inside her, and every few minutes a twinge would make her double over and breathe in and out until it stopped. She'd also outgrown everything except the sweat pants she'd gotten from the Village Discount. Her legs were swollen, she had stretch marks, her belly button stuck out, and although she was peeing all the time, she hadn't done a number two in days.

"Terrell, leave me alone!" He whined about wanting his mama. "Well, Mama ain't here, so you listen to me!" He rubbed his snotty face on her hand, and she batted him away. "Quit it!" He fell back on his butt and started to wail. "Here, have a cookie and leave me alone." Fishing out a couple of Oreos, she plunked him down on the floor and folded the cookies into his grubby hand. She wiped her brow and arched her back. "Ooh, Terrell, you're getting on my last nerve."

In the bedroom, the phone rang, so she lumbered over to get it. "Come with me, Terrell."

It was her friend, Shawna, calling to report that Jabarri had hooked up with Renée. Thanks, Bitch. She was about to shut Shawna down when she heard a crash in the kitchen. Dropping the receiver, she rushed in and saw Terrell on his back, screaming, waving his arms and legs all around, spaghetti caught in his clothes and hair.

"Kaiesha! Come here! Get me a towel."

She hoisted Terrell up, ran to the living room, and put him on the floor, then gently lifted his soaking, hot T-shirt. The brown skin had peeled off, leaving pink patches. Feeling faint, she patted him with a towel, while trying to hold him still. He kicked, fighting her off, his eyes rolling, his shrieks rising in waves. When one of his kicks caught her right in the belly, she let go of him, and he crawled away, collapsing on his stomach, shivering, batting his legs and arms on the floor. She pulled his leg, turning him onto his back, and dragged him over to her.

"Kaiesha! Call 911 and tell them to send an ambulance."

Kaiesha stood in the doorway, crying. "No, I can't."

"Yes, you can. Say your little brother got burned bad and they need to come fast."

Kaiesha was hugging herself. "You go now!"

Kaiesha ran into the bedroom, and LaTendra was afraid she'd have to let go of Terrell and get on the phone. But then she heard her sister giving their address.

"Tell them the apartment number too."

"I did." She stood several feet away, wheezing in big gulps. Would this make her have an asthma attack?

"Now, get me some honey."

"Mama'll be mad if it mess up the rug."

"No, she won't."

Kaiesha brought her the plastic bear, and LaTendra dribbled honey, but it was hard to spread it on the burned skin. His voice was hoarse from screaming, and she wrapped him again in the towel, hugging his back to her belly so he couldn't kick her again, holding him tight until her arms ached, rocking him.

"Ssh, Terrell. Come on, baby. Ssh." Her heart banged in her throat, and waves of heat rolled over her.

Afraid to call her mother with Terrell screaming in the background, she waited until the paramedics came. They strapped him to a board and listened to his heart. One of them asked if LaTendra was the mother.

"She's at work." The man shook his head and muttered something about Child Services.

She called and the nursing home paged her mother, who took a few minutes to come to the phone. LaTendra told her that Terrell pulled the pan off the stove when she turned her back.

"Why weren't you watching him? You know he get into everything. Oh, my baby."

LaTendra, who was only fifteen, thought, I'm your baby too.

"I put honey on his skin, Mama."

"That won't do no good if he's burned bad."

"Mama, I'm sorry. It was an accident."

But her mother asked to talk to the paramedic, so LaTendra didn't get a chance to tell her mother she'd get Kaiesha off to school in the morning.

After the paramedics left with Terrell, Kaiesha cried, asking for her brother, and LaTendra tried to give her a hug, but she swatted at her. LaTendra wrapped her into a hug.

"It's okay, Kaiesha. Terrell is with the doctors. And Mama is going there now."

"I want Mama here."

"I do too. Let's go lay in bed and take our animals with us."

She piled stuffed animals and dolls on their mother's bed and put Kaiesha in the middle.

Kaiesha grabbed the Barbie and started undressing her as LaTendra stripped off her own clothes and crawled under the covers with her sister. Her back hurt, and pains ran down her legs. She propped pillows behind her head so she wouldn't burp up a sour taste.

Although she hadn't eaten, LaTendra felt like throwing up. Cramps rippled across her belly, so she rolled onto her side. LaTendra took the barrettes out of Kaiesha's hair and stroked her head.

"Go to sleep. I'll wake you up when we know something."

Every time she closed her eyes, she saw Terrell on the floor, his arms and legs twitching. And heard his screams. How was she going to take care of her own baby when she let this happen to Terrell?

At about midnight, the phone rang. Her mother was at Children's Hospital with Terrell and said that they'd put him in isolation and had given him medicine for the pain.

"They don't know nothing yet, but his face and chest are real bad. I'm just praying."

"I'm sorry, Mama."

"Yeah? Too late for sorry." And she hung up.

In the morning, Kaiesha asked why LaTendra got to stay home from school and she didn't.

"I have to wait for Mama."

"I don't want to go to school."

"You have to do what I say. I'm in charge."

"I'm telling Mama."

"Go ahead." Her belly really hurt now. Throwing a coat over her sweat pants and top, she walked Kaiesha to the corner, where a crossing guard stopped traffic for school kids. Kaiesha clung to her legs.

"You gotta go," LaTendra said. "I can't babysit you today."

Kaiesha gave her a dirty look but followed the others across the street.

Back at the apartment, LaTendra sank onto the floor in front of the TV, closed her eyes and felt herself drift off to sleep.

She woke up in a puddle, so she rolled onto her hands and knees, then crawled to the bathroom. Stripping off her underwear, she sat on the toilet, but a terrible cramp started, and she had to stop and lean over, her hands on her knees. She inched over to the sink and splashed some water between her legs. More water spilled out. She knew the baby was coming.

Because the birth classes took place at night, she couldn't go, and she hadn't seen a doctor, so she didn't know her due date. Mama was furious at LaTendra for getting pregnant, just like she did, at fifteen.

"Didn't you learn nothing from me? How'm I going to pay for a baby?"

But she wanted her mother there. Should she call an ambulance? How would they pay for it? As she was crawling to the phone, another cramp took hold, and she tried breathing, but it didn't help. Up on her hands and knees, she panted, screaming when the pain got bad. Her body felt like a rag someone was squeezing. Between the cramps, she put her face on the cool tiles of the bathroom floor. The pains came faster and got worse and barely gave her time to rest between them. At one point, she felt like she had to do a number two, so she pulled herself up to the toilet and sat down. But she felt the baby push hard, and she slipped back to the floor, crying for her mama. She felt herself rip down below, and she screamed and screamed until her throat hurt. Finally, the baby pushed out of her and she fell back, sobbing. After a moment, she looked and saw the baby wiggling on the floor, then heard it start to cry. She inched around to look at the baby, covered with blood and sticky stuff with a big purple hose coming out its belly button and back into LaTendra's body. She lifted the cord and saw that the baby was a girl. Wailing, the baby was shivering, her legs pulled up to her belly. LaTendra grabbed a towel and wrapped her up, putting the baby on her own belly. Then she had more cramps and felt something slip out of her, a blob attached to the end of the hose. She'd heard about it, the placenta. After a moment, she held the baby to her breast because that's what new mothers do.

When she was sure the cramps had finally stopped, she dragged herself to her feet and got a washcloth to clean the baby up. So small. Her skin was light, but she knew from when Terrell got born that black babies start that way and darken up later. Jabarri was darker than LaTendra. Since she wouldn't ever know her daddy, LaTendra hoped the baby would look more like her. Seeing the baby on the floor made her think of Terrell twitching, and she shut her eyes.

LaTendra cuddled her baby for a while, but the floor was cold, so she sat on the toilet. Her bottom ached where the baby tore her. Stuffing two pads in clean underwear, she lifted the baby with the placenta and staggered toward her bed. They slept for a while until the baby woke her up, crying. LaTendra held the baby to her breast and felt the tiny lips start to suck. The cord with the nasty placenta made her feel sick, so she kept it wrapped up in a towel. After she rested for a while, she'd go to the emergency room, where the doctor could cut it off the baby's belly. She'd already chosen the name LaToya. Her skin was kind of wrinkled, but she had beautiful little hands and feet.

In the kitchen, she swiped at the worst of the mess but had to stop because she nearly fainted. What if Terrell didn't survive? Would he have scars? Would her mother ever forgive her?

Back in the bedroom, she fell asleep next to LaToya, then woke up with a start, afraid that she'd rolled over and smothered her. LaTendra clawed at the covers, found the baby under a fold of the blanket, and burst into tears. What if she dropped LaToya? What if she burned her? How would she and her mother handle three children?

LaTendra grabbed sweatpants and a sweater from a pile on the floor. She sat in a chair with LaToya, staring at her, running a finger along her cheek. LaToya had big, wide-spaced eyes and little ears that sat flat against her head. Good, at least she didn't get Jabarri's big ones.

LaTendra worried she'd been born too early, and they couldn't afford more doctors' bills, especially with Terrell in the hospital. She took the pink blanket she'd bought for the baby and wrapped her and the placenta up so that just her face showed.

"I love you, LaToya," she said, kissing her. The baby had started to cry again, her mouth quivering. "Ssh, baby. Ssh."

She stuffed her feet into tight boots, then zipped LaToya and the placenta in a towel under her coat to look like a baby bump. Careful to wait until no one was standing out front, she left the building. Snow was falling, and the wind blew. Weiss Memorial, the nearest hospital, was several stops away. She walked to the bus stop and looked north, stamping her feet, hugging LaToya under her coat, making sure the baby had room to breathe. Her legs still felt shaky and the cold hurt her sore bottom. After ten minutes, the bus still hadn't come, so she decided to duck into the Catholic church to rest and get warm.

Although she walked by this church all the time, she'd never been inside. Her mother had grown up Baptist, and they went a few times at Christmas and Easter to her grandmother's church on the South Side, but after she passed, they stopped going.

LaTendra climbed the stairs and pulled open two sets of heavy wooden doors. Inside, a long, high ceiling crisscrossed at the front and colored windows ran down the walls like ribbons.

Inside the door, there was a tray of electric candles, half of them lit. An old white lady stood in front of the candles, and she pulled a wrinkled dollar bill from her pocket and stuffed it into the box, then she pushed a button to light a candle. Over the candles hung a painting of Mary holding up baby Jesus, balancing him on one hand, gold shooting out of their heads. He looked like a little man, not small and fragile like LaToya. LaTendra wondered if she should buy a candle for Terrell, but she didn't have money. It must be the honor system because no one was watching to make sure you paid. What did those candles do anyway? Would they make Terrell better? She didn't think so.

LaTendra saw a big stone bowl with water in it. A Mexican lady pushed past her and dipped her fingers in the water, then crossed herself before walking down the long aisle. An old man with a walker wheezed up and did the same thing. LaTendra stuck her pinkie into the water and unzipped her jacket, touching LaToya's forehead with her damp finger.

She walked down the aisle and sank down on one of the benches, stretching out her feet and looking up. From the outside, the church didn't look big, but this tall ceiling made her dizzy. Two rows up, a man, down on his knees, mumbled under his breath, crossed himself and sat on the bench.

She closed her eyes and leaned her head back, but LaToya started to cry, and LaTendra was afraid of getting in trouble for bringing a baby to church. She saw a little wooden house with two doors. It said Confessional. She slipped into the wooden house and closed the door behind her. The smell of polish made her nose stuff up. LaToya was working herself up into a good cry, and LaTendra sat, bouncing the baby, but it hurt so she started to cry herself.

"Please, stop, LaToya."

She unzipped her jacket, lifted her shirt, and took LaToya out, putting the baby up to her breast. LaToya pinched her lips on LaTendra's nipple and that stopped the crying. It hurt though, and she could feel herself leak into the pad.

She'd heard from Shawna that Catholics could tell their sins to the priest, and they would go away. She wanted to confess that she'd let Terrell get burned and that she was scared of being a bad mother. At the hospital, she knew they'd ask her a lot of questions. Maybe they'd be mad at her for letting the baby get born at home. Was she supposed to cut the cord herself? But what if she had, and LaToya had started to bleed? What if it was too late to cut the cord and LaToya had to wear it around all the time? Would they call Child Services on her? Her bottom hurt so much, and she was afraid she'd bleed too much and pass out. But the box was warm, and she couldn't bear taking LaToya out in the cold again. All she wanted was to go back home and sleep.

The music had started, and LaToya knew there'd be more people in the church. She was afraid the priest would find her in the little house and get mad at her. It was warm in the wooden house. The baby would be safe. Someone would find her and take her to the hospital. It was a church. The painting with the baby-man Jesus. All those people who were praying for someone. Maybe they would pray for LaToya.

The baby had fallen asleep again, and LaTendra kissed her several times on the head and wrapped the cloth around her, placing her on the low bench. She said, "I'm sorry, LaToya," before leaving the wooden house, slipping out the front door and into the street.

Alewives

Susan drove Paul to the train and as he kissed her, the strength left her body.

"Have a good day," he said and smiled. "Get out and do something fun."

He headed down the steps, his coffee and paper in hand, to the train that would take him to Chicago, to a life Susan knew was more real than her own.

She couldn't go home just yet. The house was too big, too empty, full of unused bedrooms. So she drove around town, past the apartments located upstairs from the pricey boutiques and the stucco bungalows near the village center, up curving streets, down quiet, tree-lined lanes, past the new-money houses built on tear-down lots and the old-money mansions on Sheridan along the shore of Lake Michigan. With the sun in her eyes, she opened her window and smelled the piles of dead, stinking alewives choking the lakefront—nature gone berserk—and she was glad that the rich had the worst of the stench. She closed the window, but the smell was in her bones and she couldn't leave it behind her. This town buzzed with fertility—fish in the lake, deer in the forest preserve, pregnant women pushing babies in strollers and dreaming of another baby in two years.

Children with backpacks were assembling on the curbs, waiting for the school bus while moms in tennis skirts lugged recycling bins, piled high with juice and mineral water bottles, the vodka and Chardonnay empties tucked discreetly underneath. These women knew what to keep and what to throw away.

What would she do with her days now that she'd given up the idea of children?

"Join a bridge group, the Junior League," Paul said. "Redecorate the house; you're artistic. You have all day to do what you want. I envy you."

Most days she didn't have the strength to change out of her nightgown and robe until it was time to go pick him up at the station.

The crossing guard held her STOP sign aloft to let through a stream of school kids with their neon-colored bike helmets. Healthy lunches had been fixed, permission slips signed, play-dates arranged, lessons scheduled, cheeks kissed. All was in order here.

She headed her car toward the expressway. It was backed up with commuters, people with things to do, people who needed the road, so she turned around and drove toward the lake again. Driving past the tennis club, she saw the clusters of women warming up, and felt a pinch of anger at their easy lives—kids in place, houses neat, friends in rectangles of four.

On Green Bay Road, black housekeepers and grocery clerks got off the northbound bus on their way to work. She passed trucks filled with crews of Hispanic men heading to groom the North Shore lawns. As she entered the city, she saw black and brown children playing in schoolyards, chasing each other, scuffling in the dust.

Heading south on the Outer Drive, she stared at the reflection of the sun on the lake until she was blinded, then closed her eyes for a moment and blue clouds replaced the white ones behind her eyelids. She wished she could drive out onto the surface of the lake, smooth as a mirror, look deep into the water and find herself. The highway curved along past the Ferris wheel at Navy Pier, and the boats in the harbor. The skyline of Chicago was to her right. Paul was there, hunched over actuarial tables, calculating risks, not thinking of her.

She passed the turn-off for the Art Institute, where she'd gone so many times to stand in front of the Chinese tapestries, to sit and breathe in the blue of the Chagall windows, blue as the Mediterranean. She'd gone to the miniature Thorne Rooms once but hated them, imagining she was trapped in one, a doll frozen with a tray of martinis, a metal shaker in her hand, and a roast in the oven.

She hated to shop. She had too many things already, too much money, too much security, more than she ever thought she'd have, growing up. There were women everywhere, women dressed to shop as if shopping were a job, a career. Women dressing up to have lunch, to do the job of lunch. Women, busy at their tasks.

What did she want now that children weren't possible? A job? Doing what? She'd been an art major in college. A painter. Paul wanted her to join a painting class at the Community House, but she'd seen those paintings of nice, pretty flowers, of sweet children, of brightly colored houses. The impulse to splash black paint all over them scared her.

Past the Loop, she drove west on Taylor, turned south on Ashland. When she saw signs in Spanish, she knew she'd reached Pilsen. She drove around the dusty streets strewn with trash until she saw a painted concrete viaduct. The murals blended, one into the next: panels stressing neighborhood cooperation; overlapping profiles of multiple colors—brown, tan, black, even pastels—all looking in the same direction; murals to Che Guevara; murals where the grotesque and fanciful mingled—some stylized, some realistic.

She stopped in front of one long horizontal panel in whose upper half floated Aztec ancestors in full costume above the present-day Mexican-American descendants working in the bottom half—building houses, preparing food, tending to children. Around the border, skulls and skeletons danced, and in the center sat a woman with a brilliant flower growing from her head and a cut-away abdomen, a curled-up fetus visible within her womb. Susan stared at the mural for a long time, wishing she could enter this painting, become this woman, penetrate her mystery. She wanted to run her hands over the paint, and even opened the door before remembering she was still in her nightgown and robe.

Settled back in her seat, she imagined painting her own mural, swinging brushes broadly and boldly, dipping her arms up to the elbows in bright colors and swirling and smearing, mixing them, scraping her knuckles on the bricks, painting a huge, frightening figure, a Medusa, a woman, radiant and glowing, a woman turned inside out, her uterus red and raw, exposed, its hostile territory, its inhospitable landscape, its rocky slopes where nothing living could cling, which would reject, slough off, abort. The woman was exposed much like Susan at her doctor's, trussed up in the stirrups—her empty uterus, big enough for a crowd but empty and echoing. She'd like to perform her painting on the walls of the houses in her town—women with flaming hair and fire coming from their fingers; women who ovulate, abort, menstruate. Surprise art. Guerilla art. She'd leave her mark. No one would know she'd done it.

She felt pressure on her bladder and realized she needed to pee. She was a good forty-five minutes from home. Her blue velour robe wouldn't pass for a coat, especially with the slippers, so she couldn't walk into a fast food place. She searched her car for a cup but didn't find one. When she pulled away from the curb, she heard the crunch of a bottle, then a psssst sound and knew her tire had blown. After sitting a minute, she took out her cell phone and called Paul's work number. His assistant answered but said he was at a meeting and would be tied up for hours.

"No message," Susan said.

Hoping for a gas station, she drove slowly, the car bumping along. Fearing she was doing damage to the wheel rim, she pulled to the curb again, and put the car in park. She looked around for people and, seeing none, stepped out of the car, darting beneath a viaduct into a dark corner where she pulled down her underpants, crouched, and let the pee stream out, praying she wouldn't be discovered. On the ground in front of her feet lay a used condom. Standing up, she felt a line of urine run down her leg into her slipper, and she wiped it with her robe, wondering how long it would be before she'd be home again, showering.

Back at her car, a man was inspecting the tire. He looked about forty years old, strongly built, with a leonine head of hair. She could detect the Aztec ancestry in his face.

"*Señora, la llanta, no está bien,*" he said, pointing. She shrugged, pulling her robe tightly around her. He looked at her slippers, then back to the tire. "*¿Tienes un gato?*"

What, a cat? she thought. She shook her head and then he pantomimed the action of jacking up the car. "Oh, a jack. No, that's okay."

He twisted his wrist in a key-opening gesture and then pointed to the trunk. Finally, she opened the trunk and let him find what he needed, though she imagined him stealing the car or mugging her when he was finished.

He took off his jacket and crouched to begin working on the car. He seemed to know what he was doing as he lifted off the old tire and replaced it with the spare.

Susan sat on the curb and watched, wrapping the panels of her robe around her legs, and kicking at the trash in the gutter.

"*¿Le pasa algo?*" He pointed to her robe. "*¿Quiere escaparse?*"

"No, just driving around." She pantomimed hands on the steering wheel and then pointed at her watch. "I lost track of time." She could tell he didn't believe her.

"*¿Por qué este mural?*" He mimicked looking at the mural by putting his hands up like binoculars.

"*Yo,* uh, *artista.*" Groping for words, she wielded an imaginary brush in the air.

"*Ay, que bueno. ¿*You are *pintora famosa?*"

"No, not famous." She laughed, but it felt good to tell someone that she was an artist.

He smiled. "*Mañana famosa.*" He stood up. "*Ya,*" dusting his hands off on his pants. "Drive careful."

She fumbled in her purse to find money to pay him.

"No, no," he said. She pressed some toward him. "*No, gracias.*"

"*Gracias,* thank *you.*" She pulled herself up, careful to keep her robe closed. He offered a hand, hard with callouses and covered with car dust. She resisted the urge to dust off her hand. "Bye, *adios,*" she said as she drove away, shaking.

She took the expressway back north, past the Loop, past the housing projects, and soon, was back to the trees and grass of the North Shore. The closer she got to her exit, though, the tighter the bands of steel pulled around her chest. By the time she reached her house, she was nearly breathless. She could barely drag herself inside, where she fell into a chair, sweaty and exhausted. Finally, she willed herself to take a shower and get dressed. She needed to go to the hardware store before she picked Paul up.

At six-fifteen, Susan pulled her car into line behind the other shiny cars, minivans, and Jeeps with license plates like MOMS CAB, and bumper stickers advertising their honor students, soccer players, or their financial support for pandas. Across the street was the coffee house, where the Cub Scouts had painted the windows for Halloween—orange, green, and brown monsters, white ghosts, smeared on the panes in poster paint, dripping, messy. Susan liked the temporary disorder these paintings created. When Paul came up the stairs from the train, she closed the paper bag she'd bought at the hardware store.

That night, she waited until Paul was emitting little puffing noises. She slipped out of bed and pulled on the black sweats she'd laid out in the guest room before going to bed. Driving to the center of town, she parked a block away from the square. All signs were tastefully written in script or Gothic lettering. Even the McDonald's was hidden in a fake Tudor building.

As she opened her car door, the fetid fish smell, blown in from the lake, filled her nose. She gasped, tried to breathe through her mouth. There were tiny explosions of excitement in her chest like when she was a girl on her way to a birthday party. She thought of the rotting alewives and suddenly knew what she was going to paint. She shook a can of red paint and sprayed a huge fish, a Flounder, with two crazy eyes on one side of its head, then a Clown fish with stripes of several different colors along its flank. She painted an electric blue Caribbean variety on the window of the township offices and a Japanese fighting fish on the nail salon.

Her lungs stung with extra oxygen, and the fumes from the paint made her eyes water. She found the smell of the paint and the rotten fish intoxicating, dizzying, also the wssss of the air as it escaped from the can. The spatters of paint settled in her lungs, choking her. When the cans ran dry, she loped to her car, where her skin prickled when the AC hit the sweat.

The next night, she brought along more colors. At first, she planned to paint only the windows, which were washable, but she became swept away with textures and surfaces and found that the paint spread without dripping on bricks and wood. On the window of the fish market, she painted a Mackerel with swollen lips and a + for an eye, and waves of stink rising into the air. Each fish was more evil looking, more bizarre—dredged from increasingly deeper levels of the ocean. The paint cans tumbled onto the sidewalk as they were emptied. Maybe she could cover the whole block with fish before she ran out of paint.

In the pharmacy window, she caught the reflection of a blue flashing light but didn't stop, didn't run away. Instead, she popped the top off a new can, metallic blue, and started spraying a school of fish on the bricks of the sidewalk, the ones that bore the names of contributors to the recent street renovation project. The police car stopped and she recognized George, the officer who went to the elementary schools to talk about Stranger Danger, to tell the children how to dial 911. He had the most obvious toupee, wooly like an Astrakhan coat. She wished he had the nerve to go bald.

"Mrs. Bolton, what's going on here?" he asked. "Can I take you home?" Police were unfailingly polite to town residents, but a black or Hispanic driving a beater would get pulled over every time.

She said nothing but turned toward him, aiming her paint can

Rabbit's Foot

George stabbed the broom at his ceiling, snagging a spider's web, which stretched out and then bounced back, leaving filaments on his bristles. He shook the broom, waving the tail of wispy, cotton-candy thread and wondered if the web had been spun before he rented the apartment, three weeks earlier. The day after Celia learned about his brief, foolish affair with a colleague, she kicked him out of their house, and he moved into a studio apartment near the Sheffield El station, a monolithic, brick building populated by young singles and older people on fixed incomes.

After a cooling-off period of a week, George called Celia to try to negotiate a peace.

"You have incredible nerve to think I'd want to talk to you!" she said. "I can't believe you'd even ask me that. You haven't changed."

But I have, he thought. Just give me a chance to show you. During the last attempt to talk though, he'd noted a hint of a thaw in her icy attitude and was hopeful that he could start to make amends. There were many mistakes, he knew, even beyond the affair, but he wanted to show how he could change. He missed Celia, the fragrant air that trailed a foot or two behind her, her peach-tinted fingernails raking through her bouncy hair, her arm curved over his chest while they slept.

If the separation from Celia made George feel thick and swollen, the absence of Megan, their six-year-old daughter, was a searing stab of pain. Just prior to the breakup, Megan's first loose tooth hung by a thread, but she refused to pull it. George had tried to convince her to give it just a tiny tug. Not even that.

"You'll swallow it and the tooth fairy won't be sure you really lost it," he warned her.

"The tooth fairy will *too* know," she said, tears brimming. Now the thought of having hurt her make him ache. A few days ago, when he'd called, she'd answered sounding older already. He was afraid she'd grow up and stop needing him before he could come home again.

"Meggo. It's Daddy. How's that tooth?"

"Oh, it came out when I bit an apple. I spitted it back on the plate, and Mom found it for me."

"Did the tooth fairy come?"

"Yeah. She left me a dollar under my pillow with a note."

"That's awesome. What are you going to buy with it?"

"I don't know."

What had Celia told her? Was Megan angry with him too? He wanted to tell her it wasn't his choice to be away. George wished he could be there to see Megan's wide, proud, gap-toothed smile.

For the first few days away from Celia, George staggered home from work and fell onto his futon and slept, dreaming jagged, chaotic dreams. Since then, his legs ached, his stomach was sour, and he was having trouble focusing his eyes. The outer edges of his vision were fuzzy like with a migraine, framed by an aura of zigzaggy light. In the last day or so, he'd begun to see more clearly and so, when he woke up that Saturday morning, he decided it was time to clean up the apartment.

As George stretched above his head to make another swipe at the ceiling, he heard a knock at the door. Hopping down from the folding chair, he tossed some magazines onto the scratched coffee table and turned off the radio, tuned to an oldies station. In the hallway, he saw a young woman with straight, blond hair who looked agitated, as if she might start crying.

"Hi, I'm your neighbor, Lauren." She pointed down the hall. "Sorry to bother you but no one else is home. I have a big problem."

He closed the door behind him and stepped outside his apartment.

"I'm George. What's wrong?" he asked, leaning on his broom, noticing how small she was.

"It's my fault. He died," her voice quavered. "They'll never forgive me."

George hoped his face didn't betray alarm. Should he offer to call the police? He gripped his broom tighter, his stomach constricting in a dull ache.

She must have seen his worried look. "Sorry. I'm an aide in a kindergarten class, and I took the class rabbit, Mr. Bun-Bun, home for the weekend. He was a little listless and wouldn't eat, but I figured he was unsettled by the change of place. But I didn't think he'd die. I should have taken him to the vet." She snuffled. "I feel just horrible."

Relieved that the death involved a pet and not an elderly shut-in neighbor, he said, "What would you like me to do?"

"Could you help me with him?" She tucked her long hair behind an ear and tilted her head to the side.

"Well," George said, stroking the top of his head, smoothing the sparse hairs. "I'm not sure how I could help."

"Please. It would just take a minute."

"Well, I suppose."

She seemed so desperate.

She walked down the hall ahead of him. Delicate-boned, she wore loose jeans with a ragged hole in the seat that he tried not to look at, ballet slippers and a baggy T-shirt that said Wisconsin. Her feet turned out, her back was straight, and her hands floated gracefully at her sides.

"Are you a dancer?" he asked.

She looked back at him, puzzled, then at her shoes. "I used to dance. Twelve years of lessons. Then I hurt my knee and had surgery. Poof. Goodbye dancing." She did a graceful plié.

"That's a shame. Do you miss it?"

"Not really. I was never destined for the corps."

Megan had been taking ballet lessons for several months, and his heart lurched at the memory of her in baggy tights and leotard, tummy bulging slightly, in line with the other pink bunnies at the recital. Delayed at work, George had arrived late, but just in time to see Megan's act. He sat next to Celia, stroking her hand, and saw for the first time a glimpse of the woman Megan would become. It scared him; she was growing up too fast. That night, he'd again broached the subject of another child with Celia. Megan had been difficult to deliver and Celia was afraid of trying again, even though they'd always talked of having more children.

"You don't have to do Lamaze," he said. "There's nothing to prove. Just getting the baby out safe is all that counts. They can dope you up as much as you need." Celia was just softening to the idea when she learned about his affair.

When George and Lauren reached the end of the dark, musty hall, she pulled out a huge keychain, like a building superintendent's, and opened several locks, using a different key for each one.

"A friend of mine was burglarized a few weeks ago so I got scared and had all these installed. I figure it doesn't hurt to be safe."

She screwed her mouth into a crooked smile, and George wondered if she lived alone. Of course she must or she wouldn't be asking him for help.

She pushed open the door and motioned for him to enter. George realized with a twinge of guilt that the last woman's apartment he'd visited had been his one-night stand. On Lauren's walls hung art prints. He recognized one, a Picasso line drawing of a hand holding a simple bouquet of flowers. On the floor sat puffy beanbag chairs, and the coffee table held an arrangement of dried flowers in a lumpy, ceramic vase. Crumpled in a wad on the coffee table lay a bra and a pair of tights. Lauren scooped them up and rolled them into a ball, stuffing them behind a cushion. George looked for signs of a man's presence—a discarded *Sports Illustrated*, dirty crew socks.

"Sorry," Lauren said. "This place is a pit. School has kept me really busy."

"I'm no housekeeper myself," he said, embarrassed that he'd intruded on her privacy, although she'd asked *him*, hadn't she?

Her apartment reminded him a little of Celia's during their early days together. They'd met in graduate school, where he'd mooned after her, an unattainable goal. She'd surprised him first by accepting his dates, then by announcing, after a few passionate couplings, that they should move in together. They married right after graduation, nearly eight years ago. In his living room was the now-stained couch, salvaged from their basement, where they'd drunk dark beers and eaten greasy burgers, before Celia gave up red meat, and where they'd first made love, laughing, knocking over a bottle of beer in their haste. They'd lie there afterwards, their heads at either end of the couch, their legs intertwined, reading, or trying to, during the spring semester. As the year-end approached, George had imposed a limit on their time together so he could finish his thesis. In those days, they couldn't keep their hands off each other. What had happened? Did he miss the newness of their passion?

"Oh, my. What should we do?" He inspected the opening to the cage. "Do you have an extra-large garbage bag? Like for lawn clippings maybe? When does the garbage go out?"

"You're not going to dump him are you?"

"Well, I figured that would be the easiest way to deal with it."

"Oh, no. I couldn't tell the children that he went into a dumpster. I never lie to them." He wondered how the children would know where the rabbit ended up but he decided not to push it, remembering Megan's brief ownership of a white mouse, which she'd pestered them about for months. After they broke down and bought one, she promptly lost interest and neglected it, leaving Celia to feed it and clean the cage. When it died, George flushed it down the toilet but told Megan the mouse had run away. Now he felt guilty about lying. Maybe he'd offer her a new one for her birthday.

"I was hoping you'd bury him for me," Lauren said.

George thought about the unsavory prospect of burying this behemoth and didn't know how she would handle it herself.

"Bury it? Where? It's a long way to the forest preserve."

"I was thinking of that little plot of land behind the building."

"The patio? Aren't there rules about digging here?"

"Nobody's going to see or care. By spring, it'll have grown over. It won't take long, I'm sure."

"But what would I dig with? I don't have a shovel here."

George was hoping to help her in some way that didn't involve such a project.

"I have a trowel for my plants."

She held it out to him. He looked at her toothpick wrists, loaded down with silver bangles. Those skinny arms did it. He reached for the trowel.

"Listen. I'll help you bring him downstairs and will start the hole for you. But you'll have to finish it yourself."

"Great. Thank you *so* much. You're really terrific." The cool grasp of her fingers ruffled the hairs on his forearm and sent a shiver up his neck. "I can barely lift him myself. A friend helped me bring him here after school."

George wondered why the friend wasn't doing this instead of him.

Squeamish about touching the rabbit, George crouched down, his knees cracking, and reached in the cage. The rabbit's body was not yet in full *rigor mortis* and felt moldable like cold clay. He hauled it out, maneuvering the torso back and forth so the outstretched paw wouldn't snag on the bars. Lauren leaned close to George, her hair brushing against his cheek as she emitted little "ohs" of concern. The body safely in the bag, he affixed a twist tie and hoisted it under his arm.

"You go first," he said to Lauren, "and check to see that no one's around."

The back stairs smelled of roach killer and garbage. Dust balls did somersaults in the corners as George stepped lightly down the steps, holding his load at arm's length. As he reached the second-floor landing, an old woman poked her head out her back door. "Trash pickup isn't until Saturday."

"Yes, I know, but this smells bad and I want to get it out, you know?"

The woman eyed the bag. "I hope it doesn't stink up the hallway. I hate that. It comes right into my apartment."

A scruffy cat poked its head out between her doughy, slippered feet.

Outside, Lauren waved to him, grinning, as if she'd found a perfect spot for them to share a picnic.

"Over here," she said, pointing to a spot in the corner of the tiny brick patio.

Under different circumstances, he could see them having a drink together. What was the harm in that? She probably didn't drink liquor, just wine, or those awful sweet coolers. He looked up to see if any neighbors were spying on them. Luckily, the patio faced the wall of bathrooms with frosted glass windows. It was October, Indian summer, with the air still warm in the afternoon sun. Despite the heat, the ground felt cold. The topsoil, if one could call it that, was hard and cracked. After the first layer of crust, the earth yielded more easily to the thrusts of his trowel. The tool was not meant for such heavy labor though and threatened to buckle with each stab. He reinforced the back of the trowel with his index finger. George was out of shape and became winded easily, but he didn't want lithe, athletic Lauren to see that.

"George. Did you ever have a pet die?"

"A cat got run over when I was a kid." He didn't reveal his lack of fondness for domestic animals.

"I'm sorry," she said.

"That's okay. It was a long time ago."

He wanted to dig the hole quickly so they could continue their conversation upstairs. Because she was watching over his shoulder, he didn't want to show the strain of the job.

"How's it coming?" she asked.

"Okay. We'll need a long, deep trench, I figure about three feet by two feet and at least as deep. I keep running into roots and rocks." In truth, he was drawn to the challenge. Calculating the volume needed to accommodate the corpse became a mathematical puzzle. There was no sense digging too big a hole and a waste to have to re-dig if not large enough. Why was it that women had such trouble estimating the appropriate size needed? Celia was always trying to cram leftovers into too-small containers.

"Do you like your school?" asked George.

"It's cool but a lot of work."

"Yeah. Kids can be a real handful, even one at a time." He thought about a roomful of Megans, all demanding his attention.

"I figured they'd come sit at my feet and I'd sing them songs. Yeah, right! It's all I can do to get their attention. This week they were pulling each other's pants down."

"What do you do then?"

"I threatened to pull down their pants. They laughed, but it didn't happen again."

"That's one way to handle it, I guess."

He craned his neck to look at her, and she smiled at him as she lounged on the grass, one leg crossed over the other.

"You're doing great, George," said Lauren. "Listen, I have to go upstairs for a few minutes, okay? I'll be right out." She got up and brushed grass off her legs.

"Yeah," he said, preoccupied again with his task. His wrist was sore and he'd developed a blister in the pocket of skin near his thumb. He had to reroute his digging path twice because of rocks he couldn't dislodge. His hand slipped and he barked his knuckles on a silvery stone. "Damn." He raised his hand to suck the scrape but the shreds of skin were caked with dirt.

Last summer, George and Celia had rented a cottage on the shore of Lake Michigan. One day, he and Megan spent a morning at the beach building a sand castle. Megan worked hard, scooping, dumping, smoothing the sand, her slender body bent over her work.

"Okay, Daddy, make a tower here." It was a wonderful moment for him, the best, most equal thing they'd ever done together. Celia had taken a picture of them in front of their masterpiece. Where was that picture? Would he ever get to do that again?

As he dug now, he felt his knees bent and frozen under him and wondered when Lauren would return. Megan would like her. She was in love with her current teacher, Ms. Bellini, who was fresh and open, a lot like Lauren. Her voice would be soothing to a child. He wondered how she would survive in the city, whether she'd make it on her own, and he was glad he'd decided to extend himself. There must not be a man in her life here or else he'd be helping her do this. For several minutes, he continued to scoop out damp dirt into a pile next to him, looked down at the lumpy plastic bag before him. He eyed the dumpster peeking around the corner of the building and briefly considered tossing his load and filling in the hole. However, he didn't want Lauren to find out he'd not finished the burial. It seemed so important to her.

He ripped the plastic bag off the inert bundle of fur and tried placing it in the hole but it didn't fit. So he hoisted it out and dug some more. His hands, stiff and nearly frozen, made futile stabs at the soil. Finally, he hauled the carcass into the hole and started shoveling dirt over it.

"George?" He looked up. With the sun behind her, Lauren was surrounded by an aurora of light. Tired, he was happy to hand the job over to her.

"You've been so great. I can't believe you'd help me like this. You don't even know me." He noticed that her hair was gathered up into a cascading ponytail and she'd changed into a gauzy skirt and peasant blouse.

"Well. It's important to help neighbors," he said. "People often forget that in the city."

"I know. That's why I'm sorry I have to leave you alone with this big job."

"What?"

"I didn't think it would take this long and I have to meet some friends in half an hour downtown. Sorry. I have to get going. God, you're so sweet." She touched his shoulder briefly in leaving. "Bye, thanks." She twirled around to wave at him, grinning broadly.

George sat back on his heels, stunned. As she padded down the street, the sun moved behind the corner of the building. His sweaty shirt clung to his back, chilling him. Had she planned to dump this job on him all along?

Although he managed to cover the body, the wayward paw still stuck up a few inches above ground level. He mounded the dirt up and tamped it down, creating a gentle hillock.

"Screw it. I'm done." It was getting dark and he could no longer see what he was doing.

He rose to a hunched position, his head spinning. He'd left his watch upstairs but guessed it was nearly six.

Back in his apartment, he picked up the phone and dialed his, Celia's number, but the line was busy. He needed to talk to her. Fixing himself a jelly glass tumbler of bourbon and ice, he lay down on his futon and switched on the TV. Drowsy, he closed his eyes.

When George awoke, he had a stiff neck and sticky mouth,

and his head felt stuffed with cotton. It was raining, leaden drops pelting the window. The clock said eight. He picked up the phone and redialed his home. After three rings, he heard Megan's bell of a voice. "Hello? Bradley residence, Megan speaking."

"Meggo, it's Daddy."

"Daddy! Guess what? I made a collage at school yesterday and Ms. Bellini put it up on the wall. Then I went to Courtney's house and we played Barbie dolls. She has seven. Can I get one for Christmas?"

"Well, maybe. How are you?"

"Good. When are you coming home?"

"I'm not sure just yet. I hope soon. Can I talk to your mom?"

"No. She's out with Bob."

"Bob? Who's he?"

"He's her lawyer or something. Valerie is babysitting for me. She made me popcorn. We're watching 'The Little Mermaid.' Bye, Daddy."

"Wait, Megan." But she hung up.

He fell back on his futon, his head throbbing. Eyes closed, he pushed on them and saw paisley patterns inside his lids, dark and light globules flowing over onto each other. He opened his eyes, blinking and saw the ghosts of his fingertips, blue and red, dancing before him. He turned out the light, rolled over and put the pillow over his head to block out the sound of the rain.

In the morning, he woke up feeling a heavy lump in his chest. He drifted in and out of sleep until a gnawing hunger forced him up. Nothing to eat—he usually shopped at the convenience store a block away—it was hard to plan ahead. He craved doughnuts, pastries, Ding Dongs, something sugary and greasy. He shoved on shoes without socks and a jacket over a T-shirt. On the way to the store, he passed by the burial spot. The rain had washed away the mounded dirt, and the rabbit's stiff paw stuck up above the earth, mocking him. He ducked his head and ran past.

Dust and Ice

On the first warm spring night of the year, Brian and I bring blankets out to the back yard to watch the comet in the northwest sky. Brian has just told me he's thinking of going on a road trip for a while, to stretch his legs a bit and cleanse his spirit. I know not to say anything because he never promised to stay, never billed himself as the settling-down type.

"There it is, sure enough," he says, as if the astronomers and TV commentators were perpetrating some scam. "Look at that. Imagine that being the inspiration for all those loonies who killed themselves."

"Wow. It's great," I say. "I can see it so clearly."

The tail spewing forth from the head. Bits of rock and vapor trailing behind, looking like a white veil. A wedding veil.

"Woo," he says, "I wonder where the mother ship is."

I think I can understand loving someone so much, trusting him so much, I'd follow him anywhere. Brian hasn't asked me to follow him, but I would.

I've read about comets, how ancient civilizations saw them as the portent of danger, of angry gods. They signal change, the end of one thing, the beginning of another.

Funny how the comet looks both still and in motion—held in its orbit but fighting to break away. Brian thinks it's beautiful, free-flying. I only see it falling apart. I am Brian's tail, clinging for dear life, feeling bits of myself break away and turn into mist. He's on the move and I can't hang on much longer. I burrow my face into Brian's shirt and smell his neck. He's my core—I'm all dust and ice. We start kissing and soon we both know why we really came out here.

"Hey," he says, "did you remember...?" fingering my breast through my bra.

"Yes," I lie. My diaphragm is in the bathroom drawer, left there after a split-second decision. I'm tempted to tell him what I've done, afraid he'll notice what's missing. I count the days in my head and know that my body's cycle is aligned with the comet, the stars. He nuzzles my neck and says that I'm a schemer, that this was a great idea, a celestial screw, the first outdoor fuck of the year. I feel him hard against my leg. As we squirm out of our jeans, I wonder if this is our last time together.

The air is cold, but he covers me like a blanket, a shower of stars, and we fall to Earth, bits of rock and ice and spatial debris cascading around us. He is my Sun, my Supernova. I am his moon. I wax and wane at his will.

I don't know yet, but imagine that we have started our own solar system, that a piece of him has broken off to form a new moon, a new life that will comfort me when he's gone. I'll be the source of gravity for my moon, allowing it to travel around me gently. It will feel free, knowing I'm there. I'll protect my lovely, pale moon. Would a baby make Brian stay? Do I have the strength to do this on my own?

He stands up, and his wetness on my thighs chills me.

Skating on the Vertical

Nate lay on his back for a while, staring at his posters of dead rock stars and movie gangsters, then emptied his backpack, read the algebra assignment scrawled on the back of his hand, and scratched some answers on a crumpled piece of paper. Tossing his book on the bed, he stood up. The rest of his work could wait until later. It was four-thirty and he had to meet his friends at the gazebo to skateboard for an hour before dinner.

He grabbed his board and shot down the stairs, past the den where his father was watching *Jeopardy* in the chair he'd occupied every day since he lost his job.

"What is Bauxite?" his father asked the TV screen.

"I'll be back by dinner," Nate announced.

"Take your helmet," his mother called from the kitchen, but Nate pretended not to hear her.

As Nate closed the door, he heard his dad ask, "Who is Oliver Cromwell?"

Outside, Nate jumped on his board and pushed off in the direction of town. Now that he and his friends had moved from their local middle school to the much larger high school, this was the only time he had to see any of them during the week.

His brother, David, away at Tufts for his freshman year, had warned him about New Trier, instructed him on the fatal errors ninth-graders often commit. "Don't go to the senior rotunda. Don't look too eager. Don't stick out in any way." He also gave him a joint as a going-away present. "Think about me when you smoke this and don't waste it on your loser friends."

So far, ninth grade had been true to predictions, an adjustment. His books were kicked the full length of the hall one day, and he served a detention for tardiness on another. He wished he didn't look so young—no beard, no voice change, nothing that would make him seem older than a middle-school kid.

It was a bright Indian summer day, and he shut his eyes to the sun as the wheels bumped along the sidewalk. Since skateboarding was prohibited in the business district, he detoured through the alley where, in the passageway behind the gift shop, he came face-to-face with Sam, the town's only homeless man, pushing his grocery cart full of belongings.

"Hello, Nate. I see you've brought your wheels. Just like me, huh?" Sam always mentioned his office on wheels, as if to acknowledge its oddness. "What's the word from your brother?" David had introduced Nate to Sam a few years ago. He was the kind of friendly person who struck up conversations wherever he went.

"He likes school a lot. He's playing soccer."

"Atta boy. He's at Harvard, right?"

"No. Tufts. It's close by."

Sam took a half-smoked cigarette butt from his breast pocket and lit it. He had a metal lighter with a flip top, an old one like

Nate's father had that snapped shut with a solid click. The lighter fluid fumes floated in the air. Sam smelled like ashes.

"You doing okay? You're at the high school now, right?"

"Yeah. It's all right." They stood there a moment. Nate never knew how to manage conversations and felt like he should say something but never had the words at hand. He wished he were more like David.

"I have a master's degree," Sam said. "Bet you'd never guess that, would you?" He stubbed out his cigarette and then put the butt in a can on his cart. "Tell David I said to work hard so he'll get a good job." He laughed.

"Yeah, okay. I will. See you." Nate wondered what the point was of killing yourself in school for years if you could be fired like his father and Sam had been.

Sam used to have a job and a house and family, but he lost everything. No one seemed to know what happened because he'd been homeless for so long. Some people said he drank, some said he lost it all in the stock market, or that his partner stole his money and then his wife left him. He slept in the back room of the bicycle shop so he wasn't technically homeless, but close enough. Since he had to clear out of the shop during business hours, he spent his days walking around town, pushing his cart with all his stuff. Even though he was homeless, he wore khaki pants and a trench coat and looked less scruffy than most homeless people. He had white hair in a ring around his head; otherwise, he was shiny bald and his eyebrows were dark and bushy. With a slight adjustment in his grooming, Nate could imagine Sam getting on the train every day to go to work. He was just a little dusty around the edges as if he'd been traveling and hadn't had a chance to freshen up.

Nate's dad was an investment banker until three months ago,

when a merger of two banks squeezed him out of a job after twenty-seven years. He came home one day and hadn't left since. He sat around in sweat pants, rarely shaved, watched TV all day, eating potato chips and cookies, scattering crumbs all over the sofa. At five, his father would open the cocktail hour. Sometimes, Nate found him at midnight snoring in his chair, the TV blaring. Nate didn't talk to his mother about his dad since she had enough to deal with. She was trying to be supportive, but her patience was wearing thin, particularly since he hadn't made an effort to find a new job as he kept promising to do. Nate knew they were worried about how to pay for David's tuition. The three of them sat at meals, not saying anything, and he heard them late at night, arguing. David was gone now, but it seemed his dad was missing too, as if a big chunk had been taken out of the family. If they ran out of money, would David have to come home?

Nate turned north on Green Bay Road and rolled along until he reached the gazebo on the town square. Devon and the rest of his friends were there, doing ollies and kickflips. Oren was sitting on the grass, smoking a cigarette next to Greenie, who was feeding his face again—a giant bag of Doritos and a Big Gulp from the 7-Eleven. Nate was hungry but had to save his allowance now that money was tight. "Hey, Nate," Devon said as he landed an ollie off the gazebo stairs.

"What's up?" Nate asked Oren.

"Not much. Hey, I saw you talking to Chester." They called Sam Chester the Molester.

"I just said hi."

"Yeah, we know," said Greenie and laughed.

"You guys are retards," said Nate.

"Ooh. Clever talk," said Oren.

"Shut up, you assholes," he said, laughing.

He placed his board on the top step of the gazebo and jumped, bringing the board up with him while leaning into the descent down the stairs. At the bottom, he landed the board on the sidewalk and pivoted to stop.

A group of three girls had shown up—Piper, Taylor, and Cody. They were sitting on the grass with Oren who was lighting cigarettes for them. They were giggling, leaning back on their hands, their long, thin legs stretched out on the grass.

Devon skated over and asked Nate to watch him do his new trick. He balanced on the top step of the gazebo, kicked out the board as he jumped into the air, turning 360 degrees and landing on the board at the bottom of the stairs. The girls clapped for him. He acted embarrassed, as if he didn't want an audience.

"You nailed that one," said Nate as they sat down on the grass.

"Why don't you try it?" said Devon, untwisting a cap from a soda and chugging it. "I'll show you the trick." He ran through the moves slowly a couple of times so that Nate could imitate him, first on the grass, then on the board.

Oren and Greenie were showing off for the girls by joking and talking tough so Nate drifted away from the group and practiced his moves. He started a routine kickflip but caught his wheel, toppling to the pavement. He lay there a minute, the wind knocked out of him.

"You okay, Nate?" asked Devon.

He looked up to see the girls watching him from the grass, and he felt like a dork.

"Yeah, I'll live." His scraped elbow stung, but he wasn't about to go home now. On the steps of the gazebo, he attempted the same move and this time, landed it perfectly.

"Good one, man," Devon said.

Nate loved the way it felt to skateboard—leaving the ground and then finding his footing again, the vibration of the wheels that traveled up his legs, that stayed with him even when he was off the board. Although there was comfort in the repetition—up and down, side to side—there was always a challenge to skateboarding, always a stunt to master.

"Try this." Devon laid a couple of two-by-fours on the stairs to form a ramp. Nate perched at the top, then slid down the incline. Nate moved out of the way in time to feel Devon whoosh past him. They took turns spotting each other.

After the arrival of the five-thirty-seven train from Chicago, a wave of commuters spread over the town square.

"I have to get going, guys," Devon said as he turned north in the direction of home.

Nate knew he needed to go home too but wanted to stall as long as possible. From down the street, he saw Sam push his cart toward the square and hoped he wouldn't have to decide whether to be friendly or not, to choose between Sam and his friends. When Sam reached the intersection, Greenie yelled, "Hey, Sam, you want to try some tricks with that cart?" Sam laughed and waved. "I'll show you how." Sam shook his head and kept walking. Before he was totally out of earshot, the boys started to laugh, making fun of him, laying out their manners like a rug they could whisk away at will.

"He's such a Chester," said Oren. "I heard he likes to corner little boys behind the alley. He came on to me once. I told him to fuck off."

"He did not," said Nate.

"Wanna bet?"

"Why are you protecting him, Nate?" asked Greenie. "Did he slip it to you? Cop a feel?"

"No, you jerks."

"Hey, don't get so bent out of shape," Oren laughed. "We're just kidding."

"Nate," Greenie turned to him. "Remember that squirrel?"

In fourth grade, Nate tried to mummify a squirrel carcass he'd found in the street, so he was chosen to find a freshly dead one and throw it at Amy Richter. Nate went along with the prank, and Amy's horrified screams delighted the boys. His friends would sometimes point to road kill and say, "Nate, here's a science project for you."

"Just think how he'd freak out if you put some dead animal in his cart," said Greenie. "He's so protective of that garbage. It's not like there's anything to wreck."

"No. You retards can do that. I've got to go." He pushed off on his skateboard.

"Come on, Nate. Don't be such a tight ass."

Nate couldn't return to the gazebo and didn't want to go home yet, so he detoured by the 7-Eleven and bought a Mountain Dew and a Twix bar. Through the window, he saw Sam outside readjusting his bags and suitcases. What was in those bags anyway? Nate didn't want to run into him, although he knew he should find some way to warn Sam about Greenie and Oren and the others. He just couldn't make himself do it. Instead, he lurked behind the magazine rack for a few minutes while Sam talked to Luis, the cashier. They discussed the weather, the Cubs, Mayor Daley. Finally, Sam left, and Nate skated off in the other direction. Nate took the long way home, hoping to postpone the inevitable. He didn't know how to talk to his father now that he wasn't working. It was so strange to see him there all the time. Nate wished David were home to share some of the burden with him.

As he crossed the last street before his, he thought about Sam, pushing his cart back down Green Bay toward the library and the grocery store before returning to the bicycle shop. What did he do all day? Once, Nate saw him at the library behind a pile of books. Nate peeked at the spine of the book he was reading—*Man's Fate*. Next to him sat *The Seven Habits of Highly Successful People*. Nate thought it was good that he was trying to improve himself and wondered why he didn't check the books out. He figured Sam would need a real address to get a card. No address, no job, no identity.

Nate slipped in the front door and up to his room.

"Where have you been? Dinner's almost ready," his mother called. "I need you to set the table."

Nate came downstairs to find his dad watching the news on the kitchen TV.

"Hi, Dad. How was your day?"

"Oh, fine. Kind of quiet," he said. "How was school?"

"So-so."

"Got a lot of homework?"

His eyes looked puffy as if he'd been sleeping. He took a sip of his drink.

"No. I did most of it at school." A lie, but one that seemed to work.

After dinner, Nate returned to his room. Logging onto the Internet, he looked for an email from David but found nothing. They exchanged daily correspondences, short notes about what was happening in their lives. It helped Nate deal with missing David, especially now with their dad's situation. He popped a game cartridge into his Xbox, promising to get to his homework after a quick game. Over the collisions on his screen, he heard his mother go upstairs and close the door to his parents' bedroom. After he won *Grand Theft Auto*, he sat down to do a bit of homework but realized he'd left his French book at school. Calling Charlie for the assignment, he learned the work had to be done with the workbook, so he was screwed once again. If he got a Low Scholarship notice, he'd be grounded.

The next morning, Nate piled all his books into his backpack, hoping he could do some of the work during homeroom or maybe lunch. In the kitchen, his father offered him a ride to school, which signaled an improvement, an effort to get out of his chair. Nate declined though, since he was afraid his friends would see him being dropped off by his unemployed father. Ashamed, he made an excuse about meeting friends on the way.

When Nate left the house, his legs felt rubbery as if he'd been skating on high ramps at skateboarding parks—the U-shaped ramps that rose ten feet on each side. You skated up one side, then down, then up, back and forth, in a figure eight, a little like surfing. Lately, he felt as if he'd been skating on the vertical—up and down, his stomach rising to his throat before sinking. Sometimes, it was like flying, like having control over the air, but he also knew he might wipe out at any moment, knees and chin to concrete, a total crash.

Between classes, he saw Devon and Greenie and walked over. When they saw him, they stopped talking, and for a paranoid second, it seemed as if they were hiding something. He overheard Greenie say, "I'll see you then."

"Hey, Devon," said Nate. "Are you going to the gazebo after school?"

"I can't."

"Why not?"

"I have to go somewhere."

"Where?"

"Out with my mom."

"Oh, yeah, right."

"What's that supposed to mean?"

"I don't know why you can't tell me the truth."

"Duh, this *is* the truth. A doctor's appointment? Okay?"

"Yeah, whatever." Nate turned to go. "Well, thanks a lot for including me."

"Hey, don't believe me if you don't want to."

Nate's head was throbbing, and he couldn't concentrate in any of his classes. He floated through the day in a fog, failing a quiz in French because he hadn't done his homework and coming up empty when called on in English class. Judgment rained down on his head, and the day seemed to last forever.

The next day, Friday, Nate called Devon after school to see if they could hang out together. Devon wasn't around and his mother said he came home and left immediately with his board. Nate set out to find him. He thought about his friends, hanging out, laughing, avoiding him. He couldn't find them at any of the usual places—the gazebo, the parking lot behind the middle school, the Episcopal church steps. He rolled home, feeling sorry for himself, hoping that someone had called for him. Was it because he'd refused to go along with their lame prank on Sam?

Up in his room after dinner, he checked his email several times but found no message from David. It had been more than two days since David last wrote him. He turned off the computer and logged in again, hoping to conjure a message that way. Where the fuck was he? Probably too busy with his friends to think about his brother. Why had everyone gone off and forgotten him? He shut down the computer and sat staring at the dead screen. Standing up, he retrieved a box from the closet, and took out the joint. Although he wasn't in the mood to celebrate his brother, this seemed like the moment he'd been waiting for. It was like a revenge smoke, as if he were punishing his brother by smoking it when he was mad. Besides, what was he going to do tonight without his friends? What friends?

Knowing he couldn't smoke at home, he grabbed his skateboard and slipped out the front door. From inside his pocket, his father's Zippo lighter banged against his thigh as he skated uptown. The lighter was usually hidden in his father's desk after he supposedly quit smoking a few years ago. Nate was looking for a secluded place where he could smoke. That first hit would help him slow down and relax. Life was going too fast right now. He was not used to skating high, but figured he'd manage. The sun set earlier these days; he could hide better in the dark.

At the train overpass, he turned onto the long ramp that led down to the bike path, which ran along the tracks. The trip down was so clean and easy. On the bike path, leafy and cool, shadowed by the hill from the setting sun, he found a spot by a wall and sat down on his board.

In the distance, up over the hill, the sky was pink mottled with blue clouds. He flipped open the Zippo and lit his joint, pulling the smoke in deep, deep, finally letting it out with a whoosh.

To his left, he heard the commuter train coming, the clang of the warning bells, the wheels as they screeched. He felt the rush of air as the train picked up speed and surged past him, going north. The train's lights were lit, but he could just barely make out heads of commuters bent over papers. The plastic windows were scratched as if someone had rubbed them with a scouring pad. His father used to take the train, bringing the musty smell of the cars home on his coat. A minute later, Nate saw the southbound train heading back toward the city. He closed his eyes and took a deep toke, forcing his lungs to hold in the smoke.

"Inhale, you moron," David would say. "Don't waste my weed."

Nate knew it was working because his fingers tingled, and he was melting into his seat. Maybe he could spend the night out there. He could pile some leaves and use his board as a headrest. Taking an oak leaf, he burned it, watching the sweet smoke curl up to the stem. He burned another, then another. As he stood, he tripped on his skateboard and fell, scraping his shin on a tree root. Fuck! Fucking board. He tossed the skateboard so it clattered against the metal of the tracks. He considered leaving the board there, but then he hopped out on the tracks to retrieve it. He climbed the long ramp to the street and started walking. He was hungry and decided to swing by the grocery store for some Ding Dongs or Twinkies.

Outside the store, he saw his friends clustered together in the parking lot. Nate didn't want them to see him, so he veered left. But Oren called out, "Nate, hey, come here!"

They were standing next to Sam's cart, which sat ghostlike under the lights, all metal and white plastic. Sam must be buying something pathetic to eat, hanging out with the baggers for company. Nate had the choice of either bypassing the group or joining them, but he had nothing else to do, so he walked over. Greenie was holding a blue plastic bag in one outstretched hand. "My dog took this humongous shit," he said, swinging the bag in front of Nate. "Sam will get a big surprise when he sees this."

Nate eyed the bag and the cart. Although this was all essentially trash, Sam had made an effort to organize his stuff, suitcases and plastic sacks neatly arranged next to each other. Why he kept all that junk was the question. He even had a briefcase, as if he were ever going to work again, as if he would ever have a normal life.

"I've got to get going, guys."

"Come on, Nate. Lighten up." Greenie held the bag up to him, smiling, as if he were offering drugs for him to sample. "Stick around. It's just a joke." He upended the contents of the bag on Sam's cart and jumped back.

"Oh, man, that's gross," said Oren. Laughing, the others threw fistfuls of junk into the cart—empty cups and cans that they retrieved from the trash. Nate watched them pour soda onto the cart, making a sticky mess, and realized it was too late for him to leave. So with a sickening giddiness, he took the plunge. Grabbing a broken-down cardboard box and some paper from the dumpster, he crumpled them on top of Sam's cart.

"That's good!" Oren said. "Pile it up!" Inspired, Nate flipped open his father's Zippo and lit the corner of the paper. The flames snaked up, and smoke puffed out of the holes of the cardboard. He smelled the heavy, acrid scent of burning plastic and there was a swooping drop in his stomach as if he were in midair and he wasn't sure where his feet would land.

"Shit, Nate," said Greenie. "I didn't think you'd actually torch the thing."

Snapped back to reality, Nate batted at the fire with his hands, but the flames spread quickly across the cart's surface. The automatic door swung open, and a cart peeked out, causing the group to scatter into the alley and down the side street. Nate ran full out, then stopped a block later when he realized the lighter with his father's initials was no longer in his pocket. He must have dropped it. He couldn't risk having this traced back to him.

Besides, his father would kill him if he found out Nate lost the lighter. Retracing his steps, he spotted the metal lighter glinting from the sidewalk, and he pocketed it. Half a block away, in the store's parking lot, a group of cashiers and baggers were pouring bottles of mineral water on the flames. The stench wafted in Nate's direction. Sam was hovering next to the cart, reaching for the bags, but snatching his hands back as if receiving a slap.

Nate ran home, panting and sweaty. Pausing before he entered the house, he tried to collect himself and entered by the back door so no one would hear him. But his father was standing in front of the open refrigerator and looked at him as if Nate had been in the house all the time.

"Your Mom went to bed." His father put a couple of ice cubes in his bourbon and walked back toward the family room. "Come sit with me a minute, okay?"

Nate followed him. "Dad, I'm really tired. I need to go to bed."

"Just stay a minute." His father motioned for him to sit down. "I never get to see you."

"Dad. Really," he said, hovering at the entrance to the room. "I don't feel like it."

"It wouldn't kill you," he said, irritation creeping into his voice.

Nate exploded.

"Dad. What's the difference? You'll just be here tomorrow night and the next night and every night for the rest of your life." His father's face flooded with color. "I'm sorry, but why do you suddenly feel the need to talk to me?"

"Sit down now."

Nate stayed on his feet.

"You don't seem very worried about how we're going to get along. All you do is sit here and watch TV and get drunk!" He was shouting, louder than he'd ever allowed himself to talk to his father. "It's so unfair to Mom. She's really worried."

"Nate, what's going on with you? I want you to look at me."

But Nate couldn't look at him, couldn't face him because if he did, he'd confess what he'd done to Sam. Instead, he ran up to his room and slammed the door.

He logged into email again. The electronic beeps announcing new mail surprised him. It was a message from David, explaining that he pulled two all-nighters studying for midterms and asked Nate how he was doing.

Nate read the email twice and then clicked on a new message. He sat there for several minutes, frozen, and his fingers couldn't unscramble what was going on in his head. He wrote a string of gibberish—coherent words just weren't forming. He didn't know how to start, what to say. The smell of the fire had seared itself into his brain, and he couldn't get rid of it. That and the look on Sam's face. And his Dad's.

Finally, Nate shut down the computer and lay on top of his bed, but every time he closed his eyes, he saw flames and bits of Sam's life floating up into the air. What would his father's life look like, dancing ashes in the air above his head? Delicate ashes that crumbled into dust when you touched them. What would Nate want to save from his life? What would he want to burn and forget?

He took the lighter from his pocket, ripped the *Pulp Fiction* and Jimi Hendrix posters from his walls, grabbed some of his clothes, a photo of him with David, and a few favorite CDs and carried all of it into the bathroom. It took two trips. He tossed the clothes into the bathtub and threw the CDs and a video game on top, building a sacrificial altar to Sam. Then he lit the pile. The paper started to bubble and blacken, but the plastic wouldn't catch fire. Instead, smoke billowed from the smoldering mess. Nate's father knocked on the door. "Nate, what's that smell? Are you doing drugs in there?"

From the medicine cabinet, Nate took a bottle of rubbing alcohol and poured it over the pile. The fire caught with a satisfying pop. He felt the heat on his face, and he wanted to lay his head down next to it for warmth. Instead, he continued to feed photos and papers into the fire while his father pleaded with him to open the door, to have some sense, to talk to him.

Rocky Road

Candace's mother, Leigh, is losing weight but Candace is getting fatter, so the kids at school call her Kansas. Leigh has struggled all her life to be thin, but now it takes no effort.

"I guess that's the only good thing about this rotten disease," she says, as Candace watches her prepare the nasty stuff she now calls food—seaweed and miso, tofu and bancha twig tea—stuff she hopes will cure her.

Leigh's arms look like sticks in the armholes of the shift she wears around the house. Her wig is fake-looking, a Mary Tyler Moore flip. There's no scalp at the part. Candace thinks the wig is a lie, that it's all a lie.

Leigh finished her final round of chemo a month ago—all the doctor could give her—and she claims her new way of eating will cleanse her system. Candace knows her mother won't be getting better though, that this awful food won't do any good. She needs Leigh to face the truth because she's afraid their time together will run out and they won't have the chance to say goodbye properly. Candace also needs to figure out what's going to happen to her. She doesn't want to live with her father, but what if her grandparents don't want to take her?

At fifteen, Candace knows she could help her mother. During the rounds of chemo, she brought Leigh cold washcloths and ice chips, just the way that, after her parents' divorce two years ago, she was the one who made snacks and tried to keep Leigh's spirits up when she was red-nosed and puffy-eyed in her big bed.

But Candace feels shut out by Leigh's friend, Vena. She's rail-thin and tall and wears her hair buzzed, as if she's had chemo herself. Vena has Leigh psyched up about nutrition and makes her eat all kinds of food that Candace thinks must taste like pee. Candace can't believe Leigh chokes it down and comes back for more. Until Vena came on the scene, Leigh was pretty rational about her illness, but Vena has a weird effect on her. Now Leigh has been talking about a total cure. Candace wonders why Vena had to worm her way into their lives. She thinks it's cruel to keep building up Leigh's hopes. Candace isn't sure what she hates most about Vena, her influence over Leigh or her judgment of Candace, as if Candace is the cancer, and if she'd just change, Leigh would get better.

Leigh's periods used to match up with Candace's, and she would buy tampons, bags of potato chips, and chocolate bars at the same time every month. Now Leigh never gets her period anymore. They took out everything: her ovaries, her uterus. She'd been tired and crabby for months and thought it was early menopause, but by the time they detected it, the cancer had spread.

After the surgery last year, when Candace came to visit her mother in the hospital, she found Leigh crying. She assumed it was because of the cancer, but Leigh said, "Now, you'll never have a brother or sister." Candace was surprised she ever thought about having more kids. And with whom? "I feel all scooped out inside," she said. "I'm just old and useless." Candace lay down on the bed and put her head next to Leigh's, not too close for fear of hurting her. She wanted to rub her arm, but the I.V. was taped on. They lay there for a while, breathing in syncopation until Leigh fell asleep.

Candace comes home from school hungry. Vena and Leigh are in the kitchen, brewing wheatgrass tea. Candace sees Vena's pinched lips and hears a sigh as she opens the refrigerator, which is almost completely cleaned out. She asks what happened to the milk and the cheese. Leigh tells her Vena thought they should get rid of unhealthy foods.

"But that was my food," Candace says. When Vena offers her some fruit, she says," I don't want any fruit. I want *my* food."

Leigh says Vena is trying to help, but Candace doesn't want *her* help.

Vena says, "You're going to have to start thinking of your mother and her special nutritional needs," poking a ringed finger at Candace's waist. "You shouldn't be eating that poison anyway."

Before Candace's parents split up, they had big dinners with meat and potatoes and salad and silverware. Her Dad liked it that way. After he moved out, Leigh and Candace fixed meals where they ate all the things you aren't supposed to, dessert first, no main course. They popped popcorn and poured on butter and salt and sat in front of the TV with the carton of Rocky Road ice cream, alternating the salty with the sweet.

Leigh would say, "I'm afraid you have the Morgan hips, sweetie," patting first hers, then Candace's.

Then they'd sing an old Peter, Paul, and Mary song about red, green, ol' rocky road. Candace wasn't sure what the song meant, but they'd sing in the same goofy, off-key way and would dissolve into giggles.

Lately, Leigh's been too tired after dinner to sit up. She goes into her room and reads books on wellness and falls asleep with the lights on and her wig tipped off her head. At first, Candace was afraid to see Leigh bald. But one day, Leigh walked into Candace's room without the wig. Her head looked like a skin-covered balloon. After the initial shock though, Candace got used to it. Now it's the wig she notices.

Candace tries to talk to Leigh. Once last week, Candace had just finished telling her about how Bethany Tucker had been totally harsh to her friend Fern at school when Leigh looked up and said, "I'm sorry, what was that?" But Candace couldn't repeat it. It was gone, out of her mouth, floating in the air around them. When Candace asked her to proofread her English paper the other night, Leigh said she had to meditate first.

"Can you just tell me how to spell 'conscientious'?"

"Give me fifteen minutes, please."

But when Candace came back later, Leigh was asleep, slumped over in her chair. She picked Leigh up under the arms and walked her over to the bed. Candace could almost carry her, she was so light. After that, Candace went downstairs and fixed herself a sandwich, which she swore she wouldn't do but decided it was too hard to diet with all this going on. What was the point of starving yourself when you could die tomorrow, or in five years? Leigh is only thirty-nine. Her parents are in their sixties and can't figure out why this has happened to their daughter.

Mrs. Fenton calls Candace into her office at school. There must be some guidance counselor rulebook about what to do with girls who have divorced moms with cancer. Mrs. Fenton gets Candace out of biology class, despite the fact that Candace tells her she has a test coming up and is clueless in that class.

"Candace, how are things going?"

"Fine." She is thinking about the Milky Way she will get out of her locker on her way back to class.

"You know you can come talk to me anytime you want."

She folds her hands with the diamond eternity rings and looks at Candace, who keeps her eye on the poster behind the desk. It's a stupid meadow scene with horses and trees. Candace fantasizes about a place she'd rather be—a beach on Cape Cod with her mother before she got sick.

As Candace is swallowing the last bite of her candy bar in front of her locker, Fern walks up.

"What did Fenton want?" Fern asks.

"A reason for living. That woman should get a job."

Then they go to lunch, which is the time of day when Candace most relies on Fern's friendship. She hates the lunchroom scene. You can't make the mistake of sitting with kids who are cooler than you. "Oh, that seat's saved," they always say and then laugh. Last week, Rachel Faber walked by their table with her friends. "I think meat is disgusting. It's just fat and flesh. I'd never put that into my body." There was Candace with her plate full of meatloaf and gravy.

"At least we don't barf up what we eat," said Fern. "Talk about disgusting."

Fern knows about eating disorders because her sister uses diuretics to purge. She and her friends suck on water bottles all day so they won't eat.

Candace has been having nightmares. In one, a tornado is coming and she has to save Leigh. But her blanket is nailed to the mattress, and Candace can't get her out. The winds whip debris at her head and arms as Leigh begs her to hurry. Then she wakes up and forgets the worst of it until the next dream.

Candace is upset about her biology test, which she failed after missing that class thanks to Mrs. Fenton. She really wants to talk to Leigh. As she opens the door, the shades are drawn, and her mom isn't in the living room, but Vena is. She considers sneaking in the back way, but Vena has already seen her.

"Where's Mom?"

"Hello to you too, Candy." She's sitting in Candace's chair, reading a health magazine, her feet in Birkenstocks and thick socks.

Candace starts up the stairs.

"Don't wake your mother," Vena says. "She's napping. It's been a hard day."

"What'd you do to her?"

She closes the magazine and places it on her lap.

"Can we talk a minute?"

Vena pats the ottoman in front of her but Candace remains standing. Vena asks if she can speak frankly and Candace thinks Uh oh and asks if Leigh is all right.

"Your mother is being really brave about all of this, Candy, and she doesn't always ask for what she wants."

"My name is Candace."

"Don't you think it's important to spend as much time as you can with her? She's not as strong as she makes out to be."

Candace wants to say she could spend more time with Leigh if Vena weren't in the way. Instead she says, "I know."

"It's not really my business."

Fucking A, thinks Candace.

"But don't you think this is a time to show how mature you are?"

Candace wants to pull her hair, to slap Vena. She doesn't know anything.

"I understand what it's like to be in high school and to have lots of activities after school and dates on weekends." Candace rolls her eyes. "Now, I don't mean to be critical," she continues. "But doesn't it make sense to think about someone else for a change? Leigh needs as much positive force around her as possible. No offense, but you have a real downer attitude."

Candace looks at Vena as if she has sprouted antennae.

"I don't have an attitude." Except against you, she thinks. "What are you trying to prove with all this bogus food and happy thoughts shit? What makes you such an authority on cancer?" She turns, fighting back tears, and walks toward the stairs.

"Don't go up there. I told you your mother is sleeping."

"You know what? You don't live here, so I don't think you can tell me where I can go in my own damn house."

"Ssh! You'll wake her. Come back here."

"No!" She bangs her fist on the banister. "Why are you hanging around here? My mother doesn't need you. You're really getting on her nerves. She said so." Candace feels a vicious pleasure in telling this lie.

"Candace!" It's Leigh, standing at the top of the stairs, clutching her robe, her face tired and gray.

"Mom, I'm sorry."

"Go upstairs." Her lips are pinched tight, as if holding back what she really wants to say.

Candace runs past Leigh, her feet drumming on the stairs, making the floor shake. In her room, she drags out the bag from the closet—her own stash of Twinkies, Pringles, Ho Hos, peanut butter crackers—as she listens to the rise and fall of voices downstairs.

Ripping the cellophane off of a pack of Hostess cupcakes, she stuffs one in her mouth. In three bites, it's gone, and the familiar rush comes over her. Then she polishes off the other one—cake, cream. At dinner, Leigh is still angry. There is lots of silent chewing and swallowing. Candace talks more than usual to lighten the mood. But the harder she tries, the worse it gets. Leigh keeps hassling Candace about her diet, telling her she looks tired.

"It's all those toxins you put in your body."

"Mom, it's protein," she says, sawing at her minute steak.

"About six times what you need and filled with hormones."

"Gross. I'm trying to eat."

"Okay, but it's terrible for you."

She takes a bite of rice and mung beans and starts chewing fifty times like Vena told her. It's disgusting to watch her eat like that, and it makes Candace want to gulp down her own food. Candace asks a question and has to wait while Leigh chews and chews. Finally, she blows up.

"Mom, stop! You're making me sick! Can't you just eat like a normal person?"

Leigh looks up, shocked.

"This doesn't make any difference. Can't you see that?"

Leigh seems to shrink right in front of her. Candace wants to stuff her words back into her mouth. Leigh stops chewing and tries to swallow. Then she starts to cry. Holding her napkin to her mouth, she stands up.

"Mom, I'm sorry."

Leigh drops her napkin in the trash, turns to leave and bumps into the table.

"Mom, please don't go."

Leigh stops to rub her leg before heading out of the room.

Candace sits for a moment, stabbing her meat with a fork. After she dumps her plate in the sink, she goes upstairs and calls Fern. She tries to explain why Vena is so terrible for Leigh with her ideas about a cure. But Fern says maybe Leigh wants to hear what Vena has to tell her, even if it is a lie.

"Don't you think your mother knows better than anyone what's happening? So what if she needs a little lie to help her deal with this?"

"I can't believe you're saying this. I thought you'd be on my side."

"Candace, I am."

"Whatever."

She hangs up and falls back onto her bed, breathing heavily. She closes her eyes and falls asleep. In her dream, she sees Leigh, in Candace's arms, fully proportioned but tiny as a baby with a miniature wig. Through dry, chalky lips, she's muttering something that sounds like static. Candace is pleading with her to speak clearly but wakes up before she can understand.

Suddenly hungry, she feels her way down the dark staircase and sees a light in the kitchen. She's surprised to find Leigh sitting at the kitchen table. Candace backs away, but Leigh spots her.

"Candace. Come here, please."

Candace asks, "Are you all right?"

"Fine. Just thinking."

"Mom, I'm sorry I was rude. I didn't want to hurt you. I don't want to make things worse for you."

"You don't."

She winces as she changes her position.

"Well, sometimes I do."

"What makes you think that?"

"Vena says I'm not being positive enough."

"Oh, Sweetie." She gives a sad smile. "Vena's a bit overzealous at times, I know, but she helps me. Can you understand that?"

"Yeah, but she's just kind of annoying."

"I know. But listen. I'm still here. Just ignore her. Can you do that?"

"I'll try."

Tears sting Candace's eyes.

Leigh places her papery, dry fingers over Candace's hand.

"You know what?" Leigh says, scraping the chair as she stands. "I'm hungry. Do we have anything to eat?"

She opens the freezer door and rummages around.

"Yes. Here it is." She pulls a carton of ice cream from the back. "Rocky Road. Oh God, I used to love that, remember?"

"But you haven't eaten anything like that for so long. Can't I get you some tea?"

"That stuff is disgusting. Come on. Just a spoonful. What could that hurt?" Leigh opens her cracked lips to a scoop of ice cream. It smears over her lips. "You know, Vena would kill me." Her face brightens. "Kill me," she laughs. "Oh no! I'm so worried."

"Mo-om," Candace says but lets herself laugh.

Leigh's eyes are slits as she wheezes. She dips her spoon in again. "I might as well go out with—" A cough starts deep down and rips through her chest. Candace leans forward, pats her on the back. After a moment, Leigh regains her breath.

"I'm fine." She takes a smaller bite, doesn't cough and passes the carton over to Candace who digs out a spoonful.

"Candace, sweetie. I know you want to be as optimistic as possible, and I really appreciate it, but I think we need to make some plans for you. For later on."

Candace swallows. "Oh, Mom, I know." Suddenly, she doesn't want any more ice cream. But still, she takes one more bite and passes the carton back to her mother.

Cadmium Red

One Wednesday afternoon, when Gwen's students were away at athletic events with rival prep schools across Massachusetts, she escaped to the local coffee shop a block from the campus toting a thick stack of essays to grade. Across the room, a man sat sketching as he drank his coffee. The curly gray hair, dark, deep-set eyes, paint-spattered jeans, and work shirt made him hard to ignore. Unlike the preppy jocks who taught with her at The Westcott School, he seemed unaware of his good looks. Gwen was twenty-two and guessed he might be in his forties but couldn't be sure. She wondered why he wasn't at a regular job. Could he be a wealthy hobbyist? Or a laid-off executive trying to fill his days? He sketched with a charcoal pencil, every few minutes turning the page of his pad and starting a new drawing. She stole glances at his hands, the long fingers covered with dark smudges. No wedding ring. She felt his gaze turn toward her and ducked her head, embarrassed to have been caught spying on him. When he walked over and asked to join her, she quickly gathered the papers into a pile and nodded, the blood throbbing in her temples.

"I'll get right to the point," he said, sitting down. "My name is Ethan Brooks. I'm a painter. And I'd like you to pose for me."

"Really?" Gwen said, blushing. She had a cold, her dirty hair was pulled back with an elastic band, and she'd thrown on yoga pants with a ratty Grinnell sweatshirt.

He said she'd be a great subject. Something about the planes of her face and her skin tone, which he called luminous.

"I don't know," she said, wary, but flattered.

When he pointed to her papers and asked if she were a writer, she said she taught English at Westcott. Her first job, first year.

"No way. I went there."

She brightened for a second until he said he'd hated every minute of his time there. She asked him why.

"It was *Lord of the Flies*," he said, rubbing a line with his thumb.

Gwen could make out an upside-down drawing of her and felt suspended by her feet, blood rushing to her scalp, veins popping out on her forehead.

Torn between an urge to defend the school and a desire to reveal that she felt the same way, she asked, "Why did you stay there if you hated it so much?"

"Family tradition. My brother, father, grandfather, uncles, cousins. I seem to recall some tarnished plaque over a urinal somewhere with our name on it." He laughed. "God, I hated that place. My parents made me board, even though I could have been a day student. At least I didn't have to travel far, but they'd only let me come home once a month. I was so homesick." He stared at her for a moment before returning to his drawing. "You don't look like a preppy." As a flush spread up her neck, she began to explain her Midwestern roots, but then he said, "That's a compliment." He was making crosshatched marks, and when he looked at her, she sucked in her cheeks, raised her chin, and sat up straighter.

"So what do you think?" Ethan asked. "Will they let you out of the Westcott dungeon long enough for you to come out to our place for some sittings?" Our place. Married? Gay? A cough bubbled up, and Gwen swiveled to ride out the spasm. When she turned to face him again, he said, "It might do you some good." She nodded and took a sip of her coffee, steadying her breathing. "I can't pay you though," he said, shrugging. "Is that all right?"

"Of course. It'll be a welcome break from grading papers." She lifted the essays and dropped them onto the table. He laughed, wrote out the directions to his house on a piece of paper ripped from the pad. "It's the driveway right after the big maple. If you see the A-frame, you've gone too far." She looked at the directions. He printed like an architect, the letters strong and square. After his name, he'd sketched a quick line drawing of a man holding a paintbrush. She tucked the paper into her shoulder bag.

"Wear a flowing skirt and a blouse, something bright in one solid color. I don't care which color. Just not a print. And wear your hair down." He tilted his head, appraising her. "Yes, that'll be good."

Gwen walked back to her dorm apartment feeling a giddy twirl in her stomach, eager to call her college friend Whitney, who was a first-year law student at Columbia. When they'd left Iowa after graduation in June, they'd promised to meet often in New York, though Gwen worried about safety since the attacks of last year. Besides, Gwen had been too busy with Saturday classes and all her correcting to get away. Gwen hadn't made anything like a friend yet at Westcott and wished Whitney lived closer.

"You won't believe it, but this painter just asked me to pose for him."

"An art teacher?"

"No, a local artist. I met him in a café."

"Really now. Will you be nude?"

"No way," she said, but it occurred to her that the costume might be a pretext to get her there before asking her to strip. "You think he'd want that? He told me what to wear."

"Is he cute?"

"He's older, but handsome, yes." Her excitement had waned. "Maybe he was just making conversation. What if I show up and he doesn't even remember asking me to pose?"

"You always do this. Back away from cool experiences. Dive into danger for once in your life."

"I looked like shit."

"I'm sure that's not true. And you'll be immortalized. Aren't you excited?"

She was excited but nervous as well, and she promised to call Whitney after the sitting. Trying on different blouses with a black mid-calf skirt, checking herself in the mirror, she leaned in to study her face. Luminous? What did he see that she didn't?

The following Wednesday, Gwen drove by stone fences and brilliant red and orange maples, the Colonial-era post-and-beam houses sprinkled among the newer Cape Cods. When she turned onto a dirt road, the huge trees created a shadowy vault overhead. She spotted a mailbox with the name Brooks hand-painted in gothic letters, turned in to find an enormous natural cedar clapboard farmhouse with a central chimney, a showcase, the kind of place featured in magazines. So, not a starving artist. Behind the house stood a large red barn and a garden with stalks of withered corn next to gourds and asters. She sat, the engine idling, while she weighed backing out, pretending she'd driven to the wrong address. A woman appeared on the flagstone steps, scowling. She wore a tennis skirt over tanned legs. The sleeves of a sweater were tied around her waist. Tall, with freckled skin, her hair frosted and stiff, sunglasses perched on her head, she might have been attractive at one point before the sun had taken its toll.

Gwen shut off the ignition and stepped out of the car.

"Are you lost?" the woman barked in a husky smoker's voice.

Two Weimaraners raced out of the front door and ran toward Gwen, who hugged herself before the woman called them back sharply.

"No, I'm here to pose." Gwen pointed to her skirt as if to explain.

The woman narrowed her eyes.

"Of course," she said, pointing toward the barn. "He's up there."

When Gwen turned, the afternoon sun seared a streak of light into her retina. She blinked, but the bright streak lingered.

"Come on up!" She could barely make out a waving hand and a flash of silver hair from the opening in the loft.

"It was nice to meet you," Gwen said to the woman, who leaned over her dogs as they licked her slavishly.

She climbed the outdoor staircase to the loft. Ethan was dragging an armchair to the middle of a cleared space, and she could detect the contours of his lean back and legs through his work shirt and jeans.

"You found it all right?" Laugh lines creased his cheeks, and she blushed. "Welcome to my mess." She could catch glimpses of the garage below through gaps in the wide floor planks. The smell of solvent and dust filled her nose, making her cough, and a momentary vertigo overtook her. She reached for a chair to steady herself. "Want to see what you're in for?" he asked.

"Sure." Canvasses ringed the studio, leaning against each other, two and three deep. She liked what she saw. Bright wedges of color overlapped to render landscapes: a spray of fall foliage, a red barn at the edge of a field in winter. And there were portraits: a child in an orange armchair reading a green book; a man and woman sitting, silvery drinks sweating on the table in front of them.

"These are beautiful," she said. In the corner, she noticed a large nude of a woman, Ethan's wife when she was younger and thinner, lying on a couch, one leg stretched out, the other foot on the floor, a hand draped over her sex. Was she covering herself modestly or masturbating? Her full breasts with purplish shadows resembled eggplants, her expression a confusing mix of boredom and defiance that seemed aimed at Gwen.

"That's Ruth, my wife. She used to sit for me but she got tired of it. Now she lives for tennis."

He swung his arm in a cartoonish stroke, and Gwen let out a nervous laugh.

"Let me take your jacket." He folded his arms around it and studied her. "Good, that's just the kind of outfit I was hoping for. Cadmium red would be perfect. Could you maybe undo that top button?" She shivered, relieved that nudity wasn't required, and yet pleased to be the object of his close attention. Turning on his heel, he walked over to a sliding door behind him. "This is the real reason I paint up here." He slid open the panel to show the brook below, burbling over rocks, and beyond, farmland and the modest peak of a low mountain. "That and the fact that Ruth hates the smell. She exiled me to the barn. But I have a great view of

Bram Hill, the scene of many youthful indiscretions which I won't reveal." He raised his eyebrows and laughed.

Gwen breathed in the damp, earthy smell. "I can see why you love it."

"Shall we get started?" he asked, sliding the door shut again. "Here, have a seat. Do you mind taking off your shoes?" He dusted off a sheet and stretched it over the armchair from which the stuffing had escaped. "Have you ever posed before?"

"Never," she said, slipping off her shoes, her bare feet touching the cold, uneven boards. "Will it be a hard pose to hold?"

"No, you'll be sitting, and you can talk except when I'm working on your mouth. We'll work for just an hour today. But later, we can do longer sittings. Okay?"

"Sounds good." She sat down, sinking into the lumpy, mildewed cushion.

"Just slouch down a bit," he said. She leaned back as if settling into a bathtub. "If it gets too cold, I can set up a space heater."

"No, I'm fine," she lied.

"Okay, now sit back a bit with your feet about eighteen inches apart. And spread your toes. I want you to look tired, as if you've just come in from outside and you've flopped into a chair." He flung his arms to the sides to show her, and she tilted her head back, tossing her hair. "We'll work on the facial expression later." He stared at her for a minute or so, and she burst into giggles to be on the receiving end of his intense stare. Too shy to look him straight in the eye, she focused on a spot across the room, but felt her neck grow warm when she knew he was studying her. He faced the canvas and started sketching with a pencil.

Every few minutes, he stopped and stared at her before drawing again. Then he reached for a jar of brushes fanned like a bouquet and pulled out a brush that was about a foot long and half an inch across.

"See this? Sable bristles. I have to order these brushes directly from the man who makes them in Russia. He's slow and meticulous, and it takes forever to get them. They've completely changed how I paint." He dabbed paint from two tubes and mixed them with a palette knife. "Here goes," he said, "first layer. The bones. Not literal bones but the scaffolding." He studied her for a moment. "But you do have great bones, you know?"

She swallowed, feeling her face flush. "How do the brushes help?"

"I like the control they give me. The way they hold just the right amount of paint and how the paint glides smoothly. Every artist has his own secret trick. This is mine." After a couple of minutes he asked, "So, Westcott. How's that going?"

"It's okay." She crossed her arms, then remembered her pose and put them back into position. "Pretty exhausting, actually."

"Maybe I'd have been able to stomach the place if it had been coed in my day."

"I can't imagine what it was like way back when." She caught herself and added, "I mean even before your time. Not that it was long ago. You know."

"Having girls around could only improve things. All those horny teenage boys cooped up together with no outlet except sports and pranks." He squeezed out more paint and mixed it. "I'd have been better off at the local high school," he said. "However, I'm not sure where I'd have been happy at that age. I was a pretty tormented, moody kid. The struggle probably helped me, you know? Made me more determined."

"I pretty much avoid struggle." She often wished she'd been

more rebellious. Her high-school years were spent lying low, getting good grades. Only recently did she start to realize that she should have pushed back against authority figures, taken some risks.

"But coeducation must bring lots more sexual tension, right? In my day, there were rumors of gay teachers taking sensitive boys under their wings, but now, there must be male-female affairs, don't you think? Boys lusting after female teachers? Horny masters hitting on girls?"

"I have no idea." She knew there was a lot of sex going on at Westcott between students, a fact which highlighted her own lack of a boyfriend, but she hadn't even considered faculty-student affairs. "Maybe. I just don't know of any."

"Do any of your students have crushes on you?"

"Not that I know of."

"I'm sure you're just being modest."

"No, I'm not," she said. Wouldn't she know if that were the case?

After a few more minutes, he said, "I'm going to work on your face now. Pick a spot over there to anchor you. Down a bit. Atta girl. Lovely."

It felt as if his eyes were fingers running up and down her arms, cupping her chin, caressing her head. Her face grew warm, and she wondered if it showed.

They didn't speak for a few minutes, and she felt the pause awkward.

"How long have you lived in this house?" she asked. "Sorry, should I not talk?"

"No, you're fine. My whole life. Except for boarding school, college, and a brief time in New York after graduation, this house has been home. I love it here. They'll have to throw my stiff, paint-covered body out of the loft. I'm not leaving any other way." He tilted his head from side to side, staring at the canvas. "And it's close enough to New York for Ruth to visit whenever she wants and for me to go to galleries. I dragged her away from the city because I'm a small-town boy."

He told her that generations of his family had owned the house since the early nineteenth century and he'd moved back in when his parents relocated to Arizona. After their parents died, his brother, a lawyer in Atlanta, didn't want it, so Ethan scraped together enough money to buy him out. The family money was largely gone, but he had the house and just enough income from painting to get by.

"The place needs repairs, but we're seriously house poor." Gwen didn't ask if they had children or if Ruth had ever worked.

He asked her what the romantic prospects were at Westcott. No one that she could see off-hand. She hadn't really connected with anyone at Westcott, male or female. The preppy code was harder to crack than she'd realized.

"My memory is that most of the single men there were fleeing all meaningful relationships except those with sports equipment."

She laughed.

"Arrested development," he added. "Guys who want to play their favorite sport and do their favorite subject all day long but don't want to face the real world."

"Could be. I went to public school in Michigan and college in Iowa. This is all new to me."

Had she also come to Westcott to hide from the world? "I had a boyfriend in college, but we realized we were just marking time until graduation, and he moved to Chicago, and I came here. We just faded away."

"A pretty girl like you shouldn't have any problems."

"I don't know about that."

After an hour, when she'd forgotten the cold and was content to sit there all afternoon, Ethan announced that they were finished for the day.

"Can I see what you've done so far?" she asked.

"It's bad luck to show a painting too soon. All that's there is your ghost. No eyes, just shapes. You wouldn't like it." He said he'd show her in time. "It's going to be beautiful though. I have a great subject. You'll see."

On the drive back to school, Gwen's lungs felt expansive, as if she'd run two miles instead of sitting. Waiting a week for the next sitting would feel like forever.

She called Whitney.

"The time just flew. He's really talented."

"Clothes or no clothes? Wife or no wife?"

"Yes, clothes and a wife. But since the barn was freezing, clothes spared me hypothermia and embarrassment."

"He's married, huh?"

"It's about the art."

"Right."

That night, she checked Ethan out on the Internet and saw that he'd exhibited around the Northeast and in Florida. There she learned that he'd graduated from Cooper Union in 1982, which would make him forty-two. None of the paintings from the barn had shown up online, but the style and use of bright colors looked familiar. She clicked the images: a portrait of his wife, clothed, wearing a green dress, her hair long and over one shoulder; the view from his barn in summer; a stand of red maples.

The following day, during a break, she went to the school library and looked at old Westcott yearbooks, gathering the ones from Ethan's four years at the school. She took them to a secluded carrel and leafed through them, finding him in a group photo of his dorm when he was in ninth grade, a skinny, frowning boy, shirttail untucked on one side, his hands buried in his pockets. He stood in the front row with the other boys short for their age. In his sophomore yearbook, he appeared in two photos, one of them a candid of boys painting sets for a play, the other one of him sitting in the crowd at a sports event, staring off camera. In his senior yearbook, she studied his two portraits, the formal photo with long wavy hair angling over his forehead, overwhelming his face, and the casual one that wasn't a photo at all, but rather a caricature he must have drawn himself, a fat joint in his mouth, a bush of wild hair, skinny legs with bony kneecaps and boots. It was a weird time-travel experience, seeing the same big lonely eyes and vulnerable mouth on a younger face. Rather than a standard list of clubs next to his photo, she saw cryptic anagrams such as IHPSSFM. I hate? It hurts? I hope? So he was an arty stoner back then, disaffected, alienated. If they'd been in school together, what would they have had in common? Would she have dismissed him as a burnout? Would he have thought her a dorky nerd?

At the second sitting, Ethan talked about the art scene in New York. "I can only stand so much sucking up to rich people who know nothing about art except its cash value." This was why he preferred to live in the country and paint at home. His father had wanted him to go to Yale, like every male in their family, but Ethan had secretly prepared the drawings for the Cooper Union application. "And when Yale rejected me, but I was accepted by Cooper, my father had no choice but to get on board with the idea of art school."

"But wasn't it clear early on that you were artistic?" she asked. "Even as a freshman, that was clear." She stopped, embarrassed he'd guess she'd been stalking him online. He looked at her, smiling, as her face burned. "I mean, weren't you the kind of kid who was always drawing? I just imagine you were."

"I guess I knew early on, but it took my father a long time to understand." He shrugged then made a few passes at the canvas. Wiping his brush on a cloth, he asked, "What's your dream?"

She had no idea. Being employed so she wasn't forced to move back home didn't sound like much of a life's dream. "I'm still figuring that out."

He nodded." Don't take forever. But don't settle either."

She'd been so intent on surviving the first year that getting stuck had never occurred to her.

"I'll try not to." She sat for a moment before asking, "Where did you meet your wife?"

"She was at NYU, and I met her at a party in the East Village. She said she liked the fact that I wasn't going to be a lawyer like all the men in her family." He laughed. "Maybe we were both rebelling against parental expectations. I have to admit she would have liked the security a lawyer's salary could bring."

"Money isn't everything," she said. "As long as you're happy."

He laughed, shaking his head. "Marriage is hard work, you know? Don't let them tell you otherwise."

She wondered if he and his wife had an understanding about affairs.

"Can I see it today?" she asked. It was by then early November, and he'd had to set up the space heater and had allowed her to keep her socks on.

"Nope, still too early. It finally looks like you," he smiled at her, then at the painting, "but I'm not satisfied until it's perfect."

"What will you do with it?"

"I'm planning a show at that gallery in Garfield. I've exhibited there before. Probably about twenty paintings."

"I hope I get to see it before then."

"Don't worry. You'll be one of the first."

She imagined going to the opening, standing next to Ethan as people complimented him on how well he'd rendered her likeness. Part of her wished he'd give her the painting; another part wished he'd keep it for himself. Once, he'd talked about Andrew Wyeth and his secret muse, Helga, and Gwen had later looked them up online. Maybe Ethan would do a series of paintings featuring her, paintings too personal to show to the world.

When he started each session, she'd assume her now-familiar pose and he'd stand there a moment, staring at her as he reached for his brush and ruffled the bristles. She'd never been the subject of such scrutiny. Now she was used to it, having lost the discomfort of his gaze. She locked eyes with him and smiled. If only he could read her thoughts. *Take my hand, kiss me, lead me to the couch. Unbutton my blouse. Strip me. Paint me nude. I want it.*

She confided to Whitney that something was happening between them.

"It's the only thing that's keeping me going. My whole week is spent waiting for Wednesday."

"How's the painting?"

"He won't let me see it yet. That's frustrating. But he knows best."

"Can't you just jump him?"

"No. I'd never do that. Come on."

"Maybe he's waiting for a sign from you."

The cold she'd caught early in the semester hung on as a persistent catch in her lungs, and her voice was hoarse and weak. The tightness in her chest only loosened on Wednesdays when she drove off campus toward Ethan's barn. She never felt rested or on top of her teaching. A couple of discipline problems had surfaced in her junior American Lit class. And in her sophomore English class, she was sure the son of a trustee had plagiarized an essay, but when she'd brought the issue to the Dean, he'd told her not to make an accusation unless she had solid proof. She suspected that the father's money had made this kid bulletproof. And yet, one of her favorite freshmen, a shy boy on scholarship, had been brought up to the Disciplinary Committee for a much less obvious charge, improperly citing sources on a paper. She was due to speak up for him at an upcoming hearing.

At the next sitting, she told Ethan about the school's quick decision to charge a kid who was clearly lost while looking the other way with legacies.

"I told you, prep school is survival of the fittest. God, I hated prep school so fucking much." He told her to leave while she still could, not to get stuck there. "You have to stand up for yourself. Take a risk now and then."

"But what would I do?"

"Anything you want."

But the only thing she wanted was to stay in the barn with Ethan, block out the rest of the world: her teaching, her dorm duties, his wife.

The following Tuesday, at the end of a class, she got a call from Ethan, startling because she'd just been fantasizing about his kissing her, and he'd interrupted that private thought.

"Hi. Am I getting you out of class?"

"No, I just finished," she said. "What's up?"

"Any chance you could come over and sit right now? I'm free and I feel like painting you. Ruth's out of town and I'm batching it. Does that work?"

"Oh, um, yeah, sure." Her hands shook as she fumbled with her keys. "That was my last class of the day. I can be there in about half an hour. Okay?"

"Great. Don't break your neck getting here. I'll warm the paints and crank up the space heater. See you soon."

A flush spread over her, and she hurried back to the dorm. Before putting on her posing clothes, she changed into a black thong and a red bra, then threw a toothbrush and some lube into her shoulder bag. She texted Whitney. *OMG. He asked me to come over and his wife is out of town!* Whitney texted back, *You go girl.*

On her way to Ethan's place, she fought to tamp down her excitement. She didn't want to be obvious, as if she expected this to happen, but she didn't want to miss something great either. Strong women seize opportunities as they present themselves. And why not admit this was something she wanted?

Right before the turn-off though, she remembered the disciplinary meeting scheduled for four o'clock. Shit. She couldn't afford not to go, both for the boy and for how it would look to blow off the meeting. Swerving over to the side of the road, she struggled to calm her breathing as she dialed Ethan's house phone to leave a message although she worried he wouldn't get it until that evening. He refused to own a cell phone because he didn't want to be disturbed by phone calls while he worked. She left a message: "Ethan, it's Gwen. I'm so sorry. I just remembered a meeting I have to go to. The kid who was accused of cheating. I really hate to let you down. Shall we pick up again tomorrow as usual? Again, I'm so sorry."

She went to the disciplinary committee meeting and pled the boy's case, all the while distracted, thinking of Ethan sitting in the barn, wondering where she was, growing impatient. The student got a short suspension, a relative slap on the wrist, but a relief. She didn't hear from Ethan for the rest of the day, and she wondered if he were angry. That night, she couldn't concentrate on her work so she surfed the net and played numerous games of FreeCell.

The following day, at the end of one of her classes, she checked her phone. A voice mail from Ethan.

"Hey, I waited for a while and worried what had happened to you, then I finally got your message. I wish you'd remembered the meeting right off the bat." His voice sounded flat. "But, hey, it happens. I have enough done now that I can finish on my own. Thanks for sitting. I think this is a really strong painting. I hope you'll stop by the gallery when the show is up. I'm off to hang out with Ruth in New York for a few days. Maybe I'll see you at the café. Don't let them wear you down."

She listened to the message once more to make sure she'd heard him correctly. Was it over? Just like that?

Her heart banging, she wrote a note on the board to her students, saying she was sick and class was cancelled, then she jumped in her car and sped out of the parking lot, hoping to reach Ethan before he left so she could apologize.

She raced along the road, tamping down her panic. When she pulled into the driveway, both their cars were gone. Taking deep breaths to loosen her chest, she wondered how he could dismiss her so abruptly. Even if he didn't want her to sit anymore, he should have asked her over for a final session for an unveiling as he'd promised. What was she going to do now without this? Without him?

She left her car and headed toward the barn. At the bottom of the stairs, she stuck her fingers between the steps and found the key.

Without the space heater, the air felt frigid and damp. As she fumbled for the light, her eyes adjusted to the darkness. He'd left the armchair in its usual place but had thrown a sheet over the easel. She walked over and lifted the sheet off the canvas, careful not to smear the paint.

At first, she thought he might be painting another woman in the same pose. The red blouse, the black skirt, the brown hair, shoulder length, all belonged to her, but this woman looked drawn, tired, her face long, the eyes sunken and dull. Surely, she didn't look like this. One side of her face was deeply shadowed as if she had a bruise fading from purple to blue to yellow. Her eyes looked frightened as if warding off another slap. Gwen shut her eyes, took a deep breath and opened them again, hoping that the painting would, on second viewing, reveal itself differently. No, this was her, and he'd captured something deeply damaged. He'd stripped away her skin and her organs to reveal her vulnerability, splashing it all over his canvas for everyone to see. If he'd painted her nude, she wouldn't have been more exposed. Feeling a wave of nausea bubble up, she stumbled to the sliding door, heaved it open, and inhaled the cold air. After she'd trusted him, this is how he treated her?

She turned around and surveyed the studio. On the table next to the easel lay his paint-encrusted palette, half-used tubes of paint, solvent, and stained rags. She grabbed a tube of Cadmium red and unscrewed the top. The paint was stiff from the cold and she had to warm the tube in her hands before she could squeeze out a tiny blob of paint. Should she make a big X or write an obscenity?

Smear it, wipe out any trace that he'd done this to her? But as much as she wanted to erase the painting, she couldn't destroy it. She set down the tube of paint and noticed his beloved sable brushes, knowing he could never prove she'd been there. She grabbed one, held it as if she were painting, ruffled the sable bristles, silky in her fingers. She walked back to the door, wound up, and tossed it as far as she could, watching it arc until it fell into the brook and started floating downstream. One by one, she flung the other brushes out of the loft until they'd all disappeared. Let him try to paint now.

Gwen stood for a moment looking at the sun turning red as it sank behind the hill, then she dragged the door shut and covered up the painting. She locked up the barn and drove back to school, palming the tube of Cadmium red she'd lifted as a memento.

CARBONES CALIENTES

TO SHAKE OFF A HANGOVER, Liz decided to walk to Lake Michigan for the sunrise. She dragged on her yoga pants and ratty T-shirt, laced her gym shoes, keeping her head level so it wouldn't spin. On the front porch, she took a deep breath, steadied herself on the railing, and pushed on. Swinging her arms, she walked past the produce store gone belly up, the hot-sheet motel, the private club with razor wire crowning the fence. Her eyes gritty, waves of nausea splashing inside, she headed toward the lake. On the way, she stepped around trash, bottles, old diapers, and potato chip bags. At the overpass under LSD, an egg-crate foam, burlap blanket, and plastic sheeting were piled into a makeshift nest. A rat scampered down the sidewalk and burrowed into the mound. The pile undulated, swelled, and from underneath emerged a man who sat up, rubbed his eyes, and rose to his feet. Then he gathered up the foam and bedding, stuffing them into a bag which he slung over his shoulder before trudging off.

Further ahead, a gray squirrel ran down the trunk of an oak tree, transforming itself into a woman clad in sweatpants, jogging on the trail. At the shore, a gull landed, stood on one leg, twisted its head slowly until an old man, dressed in flowing white pants and tunic, stood in its place, performing Tai Chi. A fish flopped onto the beach and stood up, a man in silvery spandex, who unlocked a bicycle from the rack and pedaled off toward the Loop. At the crest of a hillock, Liz saw a trashcan with CARBONES CALIENTES stenciled on the side. A beak poked over the top of the can, followed by first one then the other wing of yellow and red feathers, flapping. The bird shook itself from head to tail, stirring up clouds of ashes, then spread its wings and flew off to join a V of birds heading south.

Liz tried to focus her eyes on the horizon, but the sun bulged and blinding rays shot across the surface of the lake. She rubbed her eyes, looked again and saw the sun hover, an orange, pulsating blob above the water. She closed her eyes and willed her arms to sprout feathers, her toes to become claws, her nose a beak, waiting to catch the next gust of wind.

MOTHER'S HELPER

KIM DRESSED CAREFULLY TO GO over to the Sextons' to babysit. She put on her gray low-riders, tried on several tops, and decided to wear the short black button-up crop top that showed off her newly pierced belly button. The other day, Steve Sexton, Robin's father, had noticed and asked, "Did it hurt?"

"A little at first."

Three-year-old Robin poked at it. "What's this?"

Steve grabbed her hand.

"No, Robin. You don't touch people like that."

"What is it?" Robin repeated.

"Jewelry for my tummy. Do you like it?"

Kim smiled at Steve, who was looking at Robin.

"How it get there?" Robin asked.

"A person put it in for me."

"Can I get one?"

"Oh, not until you're grown-up," said Steve. "Like Kim."

Grown-up.

"I want one," Robin said and poked a finger in her own squiggle belly button.

"You want everything, dolly," Steve said and shivered. "I don't know. I'm a wimp when it comes to mortification of the flesh. I'd probably pass out."

"No, you wouldn't," Kim laughed. "It's not that bad." She pushed her hair back. "You should get your ear pierced."

"I don't think I'm the type." He raised his eyebrows and smiled.

Yes, you are, she thought.

After she dressed and fluffed her hair, Kim walked the few blocks to the Sextons' so she'd arrive before Steve left for work. During the school year, Kim sat for the Sextons on weekends, but since his wife, Alexa, was gone for a couple of weeks, Kim was hired as the mother's—well, father's—helper and nanny for Robin. She was grateful for the extra money. Two people were absent from the house: Alexa, who was on Nantucket for two weeks visiting her sister, and Sierra, their baby, who'd died of SIDS a month before. Kim wondered why Alexa had left since Robin couldn't tell the difference between leaving and dying, and she would need her mother at a time like this. How come Steve had to cope and she could go off and have a vacation? A vacation when her child had died?

When Kim arrived, she knocked on the screen door.

"Hello? I'm here."

"Oh, great." Steve glanced at his watch. "Early even."

He was attempting to wipe off Robin's squirmy hands.

"Hi, Kim!" said Robin.

A plate of syrup with a mangled waffle teetered precariously on the edge of the table.

"Hey, you," Kim said as she rescued the plate and rinsed it in the sink.

Steve folded a paper bag and stuffed it in a drawer, and Kim put away the orange juice carton and turned on the water to rinse the breakfast dishes.

"Is there anything special you'd like me to do with Robin today?" she asked.

"Just keep her from watching the same damn *My Little Pony* DVD all day long. You could go to the park and then draw or read. Nap in the afternoon. Whatever keeps her busy and you sane. I don't know how you and Alexa do it."

Robin was pulling on his hand.

"Daddy, Daddy? When's Mommy coming home? Where's Mommy?"

"I told you, dolly. She's on Nantucket visiting Auntie Rebecca." He smoothed her springy red curls—Alexa's color and his texture. "Now you go put your shoes on while I talk to Kim a minute."

Robin scampered up the stairs to her room.

"I know this all must be hard for you," Kim said.

Steve paused, took in a ragged breath, and said, "I have to go. Good luck."

Kim wondered if she'd done the wrong thing reminding him of Sierra, although she figured Sierra was always on his mind.

Sierra had died so unexpectedly and at such a young age that Kim didn't have a visual image of her. The only time Kim had babysat for Sierra, the baby had been put to bed before she arrived. Kim had checked on her a couple of times, but she'd slept the whole time. What if Sierra had died that night and Kim had been the one to find her dead in the crib?

On the day of the funeral, Kim walked into the Sextons' living room and saw Alexa standing in the middle of a group of people, talking as if at a cocktail party. She looked dumpy in her clingy knit black dress, her red hair pulled back into a knot. She didn't look like her child had just died. Without warning, Robin charged into her mother's knees from behind, nearly toppling her.

"Ow!" Alexa shouted as Robin glued herself to her mother's legs. "Robin! Stop that. Kim, please take her. I can't handle this right now."

How could Alexa talk that way in front of Robin?

Steve Sexton looked stooped, as if someone had slugged him in the stomach. "I wish all these people would go home," he said to Kim. "They mean well, but I'm whipped."

Kim fumbled for the right thing to say. She wanted to hug Steve, to comfort him, but of course she couldn't. Instead, she said, "I'll do whatever I can" and dared to touch his arm. "You know that."

With tears in his eyes, he smiled and said, "You're a big help."

She pushed back a strange exhilaration she knew was wrong.

After Steve left, Kim straightened up the kitchen and then found Robin in the family room, playing with her dollhouse and plastic family figures.

"Come play with me, Kim," the little girl said.

"Okay. Who should I be?"

"You can be the babysitter." Robin handed Kim the plastic figure with jeans, T-shirt, and a ponytail. "I'll be the baby." She was sucking her thumb and was hard to understand.

"You sure you don't want to be the big sister?"

"No. The baby. I'm a baby."

"Where's the daddy?"

"At work."

Robin was hopping her two figures around the house together.

"Who's this?" Kim asked, picking up the plastic mother.

She tossed the mother figure in the corner. "She's dead."

"No, she's not, Robin. She's at Auntie Rebecca's."

"Okay, I'm the baby, and you're the mommy."

"Who's this then?" Kim held up the baby figure.

"That's the other baby. She's Sierra." She sucked her thumb noisily and put the baby up to her chest as if to nurse her. "Kim, do you hate babies?"

"No, I don't."

"I do."

"Why?"

"They can't do anything. They pee and poop and cry."

"Yeah. Not like you. You're a big girl."

Pulling her thumb out of her mouth, she said, "My baby sister died," as if revealing a secret.

"I know, sweetie. I'm so sorry." Kim stroked Robin's back.

"Can I have a bottle?"

"A bottle? Really?" Robin was testing her. "Do you want to take a nap?"

"No, I want a bottle," she whined.

"Robin, no bottle, sorry. Play with your figures, and I'll be back in a minute. She could see it was going to be a long day. In the kitchen, she poured herself a Diet Coke, and as she headed down the hall toward the family room, she heard, "Ki-im!"

"Coming." She found Robin standing in the middle of the rug, her legs stiff and spread.

"I peed."

"In your pants? Robin, what's the deal? You're not a baby."

"Yes, I am. I'm a baby." She stuck her thumb in her mouth.

"Okay, if that's what you want, then you can take a nap like a baby."

"No!!" She threw herself on the floor.

"Yes, baby, take a nap!"

Kim lifted Robin by the elbow and marched her up to the bedroom, where she peeled off her dress and underpants and tossed them in the bathroom. Then she dressed Robin, kicking and squirming, in clean pajamas. Robin kept whimpering in a way that set Kim's teeth on edge.

"Time for bed now."

"I'm not sleepy."

"Well, babies take naps." She turned out the light and shut the door, waiting a moment to see if Robin would ramp up her tantrum or try to push the door open. But when Robin stayed quiet, Kim tiptoed around the house, studying family photos hung in the upstairs hallway. In one, Steve was holding baby Robin under his arm like a bundle. They were both laughing. Robin's wispy red hair looked like curls of rust. Another photo showed Steve and Alexa on their wedding day. Steve's hair was long, and Alexa's was parted down the middle and curled at the ends. The wedding dress was high-waisted and made Alexa's hips look fat. Steve wore gray striped pants and a coat with tails. Handsome, but his sideburns were too bushy. The bridesmaids wore ugly, shiny burgundy dresses. She found one photo of Sierra posed with Robin on their sofa. Robin had a painted-on smile, one obviously prompted by the photographer, and she was holding Sierra in her lap. The baby's eyes were closed, and she looked like a lump in a blanket. You couldn't tell anything about her face. Kim hoped that wasn't their only photo of Sierra.

Kim looked in Steve and Alexa's room, pausing over the hastily made king-size bed to straighten the covers and plump up the pillows on the slept-in side. But she worried that Steve would see she'd been snooping, so she punched the pillow back down and mussed the covers again. She leaned over to smell his pillow and breathed in a mixture of shampoo and old feathers. Daring to peek into Alexa's dresser drawers, she found bikini underwear, neatly folded. She checked the size and was pleased to see how big Alexa's hips were. In her jewelry box, Kim palmed a thin gold chain, then held it up to her as she looked in the mirror. On a whim, she fastened it around her neck, making sure to tuck it inside her top. The cool metal slithered along her collarbones, and she decided to wear it for a while and put it back before Alexa returned. Then she opened the bedside table and saw a blue plastic clamshell case. Her heart pounding, she flipped it open and found a large, tan, rubber half-sphere. She snapped the case shut and hurried out of the room.

Forcing herself to open Sierra's door, she saw the crib, a changing table with piles of diapers and sleepers, and a rocking chair with a teddy bear propped on the seat. The curtains were drawn, and there was a creepy, static air to the room, a sealed-off, tomb-like quality. She shut the door and went downstairs to read her novel.

After an hour, she decided that Robin had done her time, so she went upstairs to wake her. Robin wasn't in bed. Out in the hall, Kim called Robin, checking the upstairs bathroom, even the linen closet.

Back in Robin's room, she tore the covers off the bed, shouting, "Robin, where are you?"

When she heard faint crying from the closet, she opened the door to find Robin huddled on the floor, her baby blanket over her head, her legs and bottom protruding from the sides of the blanket.

"Robin, what are you doing in here?"

Robin was shaking, chewing on her blanket. Kim sat on the floor, pulled Robin onto her lap and wrapped her arms around her.

"Everyone's mad at me," Robin said.

Her body trembled, her breath came between gulps.

"No, they're not. Nobody's mad. I'm sorry I called you a baby."

"Mommy and Daddy hate me."

"Of course, they don't. They love you." She rubbed her back. "You're their Robin."

"They love Sierra more than me."

"No, they're just really sad right now. They love you so much," she said, wondering if it were true, if parents loved each child the same.

Did her own father love her as much as her younger stepbrother from his new marriage?

She picked Robin up and laid her down on the bed, helping her dress in a clean pair of underpants, shorts, and a T-shirt. They ate lunch and took a walk to the park. Robin was sweet and compliant, matching her pace to Kim's without dragging behind. As they walked, Kim wondered if people on the street thought she could be Robin's mother and not her babysitter. With Robin's hair curly and Kim's straight though, there was no linking them.

For the rest of the day, she thought about how Steve was getting along, and she planned a dinner for him and Robin. Robin's tastes ran to macaroni and cheese or hotdogs, but Kim had checked out their pantry and decided to make pasta and a salad. Should she get out a bottle of wine? Best to let Steve do that.

She set the table and sat looking through Alexa's cookbooks for recipes and clues about Steve's tastes while Robin colored with markers. Alexa's backhand scrawl covered the margins of the well-worn *James Beard Cookbook*. Goes great with rice...Served to the Fosters...Use less salt than he calls for. Since she was bound by what was in the pantry, Kim settled on pasta with jarred tomato sauce to which she added mushrooms, then a salad, and garlic bread from the freezer.

When she heard Steve's car in the driveway, she put on an apron and met him at the door.

"So," he asked, "did you survive your first whole day? You don't look any the worse for wear."

"We did fine. She was tired, so I gave her an early nap, but she and I went out in the afternoon."

"Thanks. I can take it from here."

"I started dinner. I hope that was okay."

His face brightened. "More than okay. You didn't need to do that. Thanks though." She turned to get her bag. "Say, there's so much food here, why don't you stay and eat some? Would your mother mind? You can tell her I'm harmless, not a dirty old man." He laughed.

She thought of her mother and the catch-as-catch-can post-divorce meals they were in the habit of sharing and said, "Sure I can stay. If you'd like."

Her face felt hot, and she was afraid it showed.

"I just can't eat dinner alone." He took off his tie. "And you went to all this trouble. You should enjoy it."

"Thanks. It wasn't that hard."

When the pasta was done, she called Robin, grabbed another plate, and sat down in what she assumed was Alexa's chair. She could barely eat though. Her throat tightened, and she was afraid she'd spill or burp or choke so she took small bites and listened to Steve talk and wondered if this was like being married. She couldn't remember her parents eating together anymore.

Kim dreaded the time when Alexa would be coming home, and she'd have to cut back her hours. Maybe Alexa would keep her on, but that would only be worth it if she could see Steve. Part of her wished that Alexa would stay away forever, and she could continue as the babysitter for good.

Kim wondered what Steve saw in Alexa. She had nice hair, but she always pulled it back so tight, and she wore such tanky dresses in those muddy colors—eggplant and olive green. Kim didn't think Alexa was that pretty. She wore glasses instead of contacts, as if she didn't care at all how she looked. Maybe she hadn't lost the weight from Sierra, but she could at least look as if she cared.

The first thing Steve did every day when he came home was to pour himself a bourbon and sit while Kim finished cooking. She'd fallen into the routine of staying for dinner, then she'd clear the table and he'd wash the dishes while she put Robin to bed.

"How's Robin doing?" he asked one evening. "Does she talk about Sierra?"

"Some. I'm not sure she knows what happened really."

"I'm not sure I quite believe it myself." He took a sip. "I had barely gotten used to her being here before she was gone."

Kim sat down and placed her hands on the table, palms folded.

"I just don't know how to help Alexa through this. She doesn't realize it's hard on me too. I miss Sierra. Alexa thinks that because she carried her, she has some keener sense of the loss, but I saw her grow. I loved her too."

"That must be hard for you."

"I hope she snaps back to herself soon. We're so lucky to have you to help out like this during your summer. You could be doing all kinds of things that are more fun than this."

"I like taking care of Robin."

"Well, she just idolizes you."

"She's such a good kid."

Kim floated home after that conversation, blood buzzing in her arms and legs as if zapped by jolts of electricity.

After Alexa had been away for a week, Kim arrived to find Steve standing at the sink, watching the water run, suds billowing up in a foamy cloud.

"Hey, Steve."

"Oh, hi, Kim." He shook suds off his hands and wiped them on a towel.

"How are you?"

"Oh, you know." He sighed. "I'm getting through the days, I guess."

"Anything I can do?"

"You're a doll. No. Afraid not."

"I brought you some brownies. Would you like one?"

"Oh, how nice. Sure." He bit into one. "Delicious. Where did you learn to bake like this?"

"It's just a mix."

"Well, they're great. Thanks."

"Have a good day," Kim said as she stood at the door and waved to him. "We'll do great here. Bye."

Alexa had been gone nearly two weeks. Kim took Robin to the park in the morning and sat on the bench as the mothers talked about recipes and their husbands and thought about what she'd make for Steve that night, the last dinner. It would have to be very special.

As she and Robin turned the corner onto the Sextons' block, they saw Alexa's red Volvo in the driveway.

"Mommy!" Robin shrieked. "Mommy's home!" and she ran the rest of the way up the sidewalk.

Why had she come home already?

Robin rushed up the porch stairs and threw open the door screaming "Mommy, Mommy."

Steve's car was there too, so he must have known she was coming.

Kim stood outside, deadheading the potted geraniums on the steps, until Steve came to the door with a wide smile.

"She's back! Come see."

Alexa was sitting on the sofa, covered by Robin, who was smothering her with hugs and kisses. Robin's face was flushed, and she was talking manically.

"Where were you, Mommy? I missed you. I love you."

"I love you too."

She placed her hands on either side of Robin's face and touched her forehead to the girl's. Alexa didn't seem to notice Kim standing there.

"Did you bring Sierra with you?" Robin asked.

Alexa shrank back, then crumpled into herself and started crying. Even Kim had to feel sorry for her. Steve scooped Robin up and hugged her hard.

"Robin, Mommy couldn't bring Sierra back." Robin twisted in his arms, shrieking. "Listen to me, Robin."

"No!" She ran over to Kim, who caught her and held her firmly with both legs and arms.

"I have to go lie down," Alexa said.

"Kim, do you mind staying with Robin a bit longer?" Steve asked.

"Of course not."

Steve lifted Alexa onto her feet and wrapped her in a hug. "Let's go upstairs."

Robin cried and kicked her feet, "Mommy!"

Steve turned. "Robin, Mommy needs to take a nap because she's very tired, and I'm going to make sure she does. Then she can play with you."

"No, I want to take a nap with her." Robin strained at Kim's grip.

Kim stroked Robin's hair and said, "Come on. Let's play with your Little Pony figures. Can you show me?" But Robin's sweaty body was quivering. "Let's sit down and play."

As Kim kept a tight hold on the girl, Robin eventually relaxed enough to allow herself to be led to the toy shelves, and soon she started pulling all her ponies onto the rug.

Kim heard footsteps overhead in the master bedroom and waited for Steve to come downstairs after Alexa settled in. But when he stayed upstairs, she realized that Alexa and Steve might have gone to bed together. In the middle of the day? While she and Robin were right downstairs?

Robin was occupied with her ponies and wasn't content to let Kim sit and watch. Kim wasn't in the mood. She wanted to get out of that house and go home. Alexa hadn't thanked her, and Steve just went off with Alexa even though Robin wanted to see her mother. Kim's ears were tuned to the slightest sound from upstairs, and every creak, every sound of voices made her wince. Her nerves were ragged, and she was getting a headache.

"Kim, no, you have to play this way."

"Robin, I just want to sit for a while. I'm tired."

"No, you have to play."

"Robin, let me put in a DVD for you."

"Ki-im. Play with me."

"God, Robin, I'm not your mom. Stop bugging me. She's home. She can do this now."

Robin picked up the ponies and started throwing them.

"Robin, stop it."

"No."

"Robin, give me a break." Kim stood up and starting collecting toys and tossing them into bins.

Robin stood defiantly before Kim, her feet planted, her fists clenched, then she hauled off and slugged Kim in the navel.

Shooting pains radiated from her belly button ring. "Shit, Robin!" She doubled over. "Damn it!"

"You said swears. I'm telling." Robin said, breathing heavily.

"Robin, you little brat. You don't hit people." Robin kicked her, and Kim grabbed both Robin's hands in one of hers and yelled, "Stop it! Stop it now!" She took the girl's shoulders and shook her. Robin's head bobbed back and forth. "You can't do that to people. Stop being a brat!"

"Kim?" Steve said. He and Alexa stood in the doorway, wearing their robes. "What's going on here?"

"Mommy!" Robin cried. "Daddy!"

Sweating, her belly still stinging, Kim explained, "Robin punched me on my piercing, and it hurt. I got angry and yelled at her." She inspected her navel to see if she was bleeding.

"Robin doesn't need this kind of turmoil now," said Alexa, her arms crossed, staring at Kim's navel with disgust.

"Kim, you really need to go," said Steve.

"But—"

"Really, this is not good for any of us," he said.

"I'm sorry. Let me clean up the room and then—"

"No, we'd like you to go now."

Steve looked angry. Alexa stood with her arms folded, shaking her head.

Kim walked to the kitchen and dumped out her Diet Coke in the sink, then picked up her backpack. She considered leaving by the back door, but instead, she walked down the hall to the front door, past the family room. Steve was hugging Robin and Alexa, running his hand up Alexa's back. Robin was back to normal, chattering about what she wanted to do with Alexa.

Steve turned and said, "Kim. I haven't paid you yet today." He picked up Alexa's purse.

"Oh no, don't worry about that."

"Come on. This is a job."

"But I don't deserve it," she said, her voice sounding pinched.

"Take it." He folded several bills into her hand.

Her face burned, she couldn't look at him, but didn't refuse his money. What about all the good things she'd done? She wanted to say something to him before she left, about how much he meant to her, about how she was sorry to disappoint him, but instead, she watched him close the door, and then she stood outside and saw Steve gather his wife and daughter into his arms. Kim stood out front a minute, not wanting to leave, but unable to stay. Then she remembered Alexa's necklace and knew she couldn't return it now. And why should she? She'd earned it. Running her fingers along the gold chain, she turned it so it glinted in the sun. Then she pulled it from inside her T-shirt and let it fall onto her chest, stuffed the money in her pocket, and walked home.

WEDDING PHOTO

My parents are standing on the steps of the church, squinting into the sun on the day of their wedding, nearly twenty-five years ago. My father's smile is confident. He's sure of his decision, eager about his new responsibilities. He holds her arm as he guides her, his new bride, from the church. My mother is looking off to her right and up a bit, away from him. At what? A well-wisher? A curious passerby? She doesn't smile. Some people might blame wedding jitters, but I know she is swallowing back the nausea of morning sickness, my six-week self nestled inside her, a secret to be revealed later. She is only twenty-four but feels her choices narrowing, believes my father is her best chance and maybe her last. And of course, I am the real reason they're doing this. I look to see if I can discern any hint of her future unhappiness, of her dissatisfaction with the marriage she finally dared to leave after more than twenty years together. All I can see is two young people, shy and hopeful, strangers to each other.

The three-quarter profile shows off her straight nose and her brown hair, over-permed for the occasion. She is wearing her mother's satin dress with a high collar and covered buttons down the front—a full skirt under a peplum jacket, not yet tight, but snug. Beneath her skirt, the toe of a platform shoe peeks out. She told me her feet hurt that day, but she couldn't take off her shoes because her dress was too long. Besides, without her shoes, she'd throw off the stair-step alignment of the heads for the wedding party photos.

My father is wearing a cutaway coat and vest. He is rugged-looking, not tall, but solid. In the sun, his eyes are nearly closed. He is twisting his new ring with the thumb of his left hand. His right hand clutches her satin sleeve, wrinkling it, probably leaving an eager, sweaty palm print.

I see myself in the two of them—my mother's prominent front teeth, the crease between her eyebrows that makes us look worried even when we aren't. My father's hairline with the dip in the middle, the wide spacing of his dove-gray eyes. Eyes that chose not to see what was in front of him all those years. Eyes that still can't see that his wife has changed. What features might I pass on to a child? How will I be viewed in future photos? What will I see in them?

In the upper corner of the photo, I see for the first time what caught my mother's attention, drawing her gaze away from my father. A flash of white. A pigeon. Not a love bird or an eagle, or even a phoenix. A pigeon. The image is blurred as if the pigeon were attempting to escape the camera but was captured in mid-flight. From my perspective, it looks like the pigeon has been shot, halted on its way to freedom. Maybe my mother only saw the flight and all that it promised. In a way, we'd both be right.

TALISMAN

SHE FOLDS THE CLEAN CLOTHES and places them in piles on her dresser, on his. He dozes on the couch in front of the TV. She sits in the dark, unable get up and turn on the light. He stares at an infomercial for car polish. She changes her pad. Her breasts are no longer sore, but she's still bloated. She listens for him at the top of the stairs and then goes to bed. He waits until he's sure she's asleep before he comes upstairs. She hears him come in but pretends to sleep. He considers waking her but doesn't. They sleep fitfully. She dreams of rivers of blood and being washed out to sea. He dreams of caves and rocks and shipwrecks. In the morning, she turns to roll into his arms, but he has already gone, she supposes, to work. He wants to call her from the office but is afraid he'll say the wrong thing. She sits at the kitchen table in her robe for the whole morning, wishing he'd call, knowing she can't bother him at work. Knowing he can't make it better.

Blighted ovum. You'll have another. Just priming the pump. It was for the best.

She remembers, as a child, visiting the local museum where there was a collection of nine jars of fetuses, stair stepping up the gestational scale, dancing in brine. Blue eyes behind milky pink eyelids, sealed shut. Nubs for fingers.

He remembers the book on freaks his friend Bruce's parents had in the basement. Bodies twisted; a vestigial twin growing from a man's chest, feet splayed; two brothers joined at the top of the heads. They'd never seen each other face to face. A man with one enormous foot and a normal one. Would theirs have been normal?

Keep busy, that's the best therapy. Get some exercise. Don't let yourself wallow in it. Go get a massage.

She feels the scrape of the speculum and the sucking of the vacuum as the doctor extracts what is left. He holds her hand and squeezes. Tears flow into her ears.

He stays late at work. She eats dinner by herself at four o'clock—leftovers and a pint of ice cream. He comes home to find her sitting by the window, in her robe, her mouth sour and sticky. He reaches to hold her. She shrugs him off. She's not fit to be touched. He yells, and she cries. He retreats to the den and the pull-out couch. She thinks he blames her. He thinks she won't let him in. She thinks he wanted this.

Estrangement is a danger at these times. Feelings need to be expressed. Both of you are hurting.

She tries to fall asleep but can't. Downstairs in the den, she peels back the Afghan and finds him asleep, knees tucked up toward his chest. He is clutching the giraffe rattle that they bought together, the talisman that couldn't guarantee safe passage into this world. She crawls onto the bed and clings to him, and they sleep all night there, curled like a fist.

Weighing the Heart

In the hospital waiting room, Mona is pouring over her book on Ancient Egypt while her mother is inside, talking to the doctors about Dad, who's been in a coma since the accident three days ago. Mona is going to be Cleopatra for Halloween, and she is drawing pictures with the correct detail for her mother to copy. The costume was finished except for the gold trim when Dad had his accident. Now, Mona's a little worried it won't be done in time for the parade at school.

Scott, her younger brother, is bored and can't decide what to do.

"You brought half your toys," Mona says. "Find something to do and be quiet." He keeps banging his foot against her chair. "Stop it, you idiot."

"Mom said not to call me names."

"Mom's not here."

"Mona and Scott." Nana looks up from her magazine. "Please try to get along."

She's Dad's mother.

Mona takes out her pad of paper and writes out a string of hieroglyphics—

𓂋𓈖𓇋𓈖𓈖 𓈖𓏏𓆑 𓂝 𓈖𓇋𓊹𓈖. 𓄿𓈖 𓂋𓂧𓏏𓆑 𓏏𓈖𓈖. (Scott is a dork. He bugs me.)

She uses her hieroglyphics decoder that came in her Egypt book. She keeps a notebook filled with her thoughts in hieroglyphics. At first, she had to consult the chart for each letter. Now, she can write most letters from memory. She loves the way her name looks: 𓏏𓈖𓈖𓇋𓂝 . You'd never guess it was stupid Mona—it looks beautiful, almost like a queen's name. At school, she writes things about other kids in code, and it's fun. She can do it right in front of people, and they won't know what she is saying. She wishes she could speak Egyptian. She'd like to go right up to someone and say what's on her mind.

Mona and Scott have been sleeping at Nana's house since the accident because their mother has been at the hospital so much. They come to the hospital after school and sit in the waiting room until bedtime. Mona didn't want to go back to school when her father was hurt, but her mother insisted.

"What will you do all day, sitting in the hospital?"

They were finally allowed to see Dad yesterday in the ICU, but only through the window. He was all hooked up with tubes and machines, and his face was bandaged so she wasn't sure it was him. He lay with his arms at his sides, the sheet tucked around him like he used to do for her.

"Daddy, make me a mummy," she'd yell, and he'd come in and smooth the sheet and blanket around her so tight she could barely move.

"Wa, ha, ha!" he'd laugh. "The curse of the mummy!"

Mona is reading about mummification in her book. She learns that the Egyptians took out all the organs before embalming the body. The brain came out through the nose with a hook and was thrown away. They thought the heart did the thinking. She also reads about the weighing of the heart, when the dead person's heart was balanced against a feather, the symbol of truth. If the heart was too heavy, it meant the person was bad and his heart was thrown to the monster Ammit, who ate it. But if the heart was light enough to balance the feather, the mummy would live forever.

Mummies don't scare her like they do some kids. They're not like in horror movies. Her class visited the Field Museum and saw lots of mummies—adult mummies, child mummies, even cat and falcon mummies. Some of the girls had to go sit out in the hall because they were scared, but she thought the mummies were awesome. She couldn't believe she was so close to anyone that old, close enough to touch them, except for the glass.

Nana gets up and asks, "Do you kids want to go down to the cafeteria to get something to eat?" Scott does, of course. Mona isn't hungry, but Nana says she will bring her something anyway. "In case you change your mind."

Mona draws a picture of Cleopatra, not in profile like in the book, but facing out. Her eyes are almond and have black rings of kohl around them. Should Mona wear a wig or could her mother braid her hair like Cleopatra's? She's been practicing with her mother's green eye shadow to get her eyes to look the way they're supposed to, so it looks like malachite dust. She found a bendable rubber snake that she plans to wind around her upper arm. An asp. She wishes she didn't have to wear a coat. This costume is very important because fifth grade is the last year she'll get to wear a costume to school. She wants this one to be the best ever.

Mona looks in her backpack and pulls out a pouch. Inside, she's been hiding special things that remind her of her father: folded-up ticket stubs, a package of mints, an old ID, a business card, a pipe from when he used to smoke, a shoelace. It's a good-luck pouch. She runs her fingers over the leather and tries to focus on fun things that she and her family did together. Mona likes it when they all watch TV, but her mother keeps wanting to turn it off.

"Family time," she says.

But when they don't watch TV, they just go off to different rooms, so it's really better to stay and watch something.

Mona writes 𓉙𓂋𓏤𓀁 𓈖𓊪 𓏏𓏏𓏤? (Where is Mom?) in her journal and wonders when her mother is going to come out and see them. She's getting sleepy and would like to go back to Nana's house.

On page fifteen of her book, she looks at the golden scarab. Her mother has scarab earrings, gold ones, that she wears when she and Dad go out on weekends. Mona didn't know scarabs were bugs until she read about them. They're beetles that roll around balls of dung. That's pretty gross, but they stand for being born again after death so they are good luck. Maybe for Halloween her mother will let her wear the earrings.

Cleopatra was the most powerful woman of her time. She loved two famous men, Julius Caesar and Mark Anthony. She loved Mark Anthony so much that when he died, she poisoned herself with the venom of an asp. Mona wonders what her mother would do if Dad died.

Turning back to the section on mummies, she starts to draw a case, a beautiful one for a king, with stripes of different colors and a golden face. Her gold crayon is wearing out because she's used it so much. She peels back the paper to sharpen it.

"What are you looking at?" Nana's voice interrupts her thoughts. "Put that away, now!"

"What?"

"How dare you look at pictures of death when your poor father is in there, so sick? What's the matter with you?"

"I didn't mean to."

Nana snatches the book from her hands and throws it on the floor so it lands with the pages bent.

"That's not my book. It's the library's."

"Don't look at that around me." She sits down, takes out a Kleenex, and pats at her eyes.

Mona picks her book up and smooths out the pages.

"I'm sorry, Mona. I'm just so worried."

Mona writes 𓀀𓀁 𓀂 𓀃. (Nana is mean.) in her journal and decides she's going to count to two hundred. Then her mother will be out to tell them they can go to bed. She counts, fast at first, then slowly as she gets to the end, but her mother doesn't come. Scott starts to whine that he's sleepy and wants to go to bed. Mona doesn't want to agree with him ever, but she's tired too. Her eyes are scratchy and it's hard to read now. Nana goes and gets Mom who tells them there's nothing they can do, that Dad is stable and they can come back the next day. Mona wants to stay because she's suddenly afraid her father is going to die. Somehow, this has never occurred to her before.

Mom gives them both big hugs and kisses, saying, "I promise to come home once Dad is settled for the night." She strokes Mona's hair. "You go on home to bed, and I'll be there soon."

"Good night, Mom."

At Nana's, Mona goes upstairs to Dad's old room, where she's been staying. She looks through the drawers of his dresser, fingering things that were his when he was younger. Nana hasn't thrown out anything. It's all been neatly stored in boxes. Maybe she thinks he'll need the stuff someday. Mona and Scott aren't supposed to touch these boxes, but she's so curious to see what her Dad liked when he was her age. She's looking for something—she's not sure what—but she'll know when she sees it. There are marbles, stones, a pair of dice, a Boy Scout patch, a pocket knife with a pearl handle, a postcard from Nana and Poppa when they went to San Francisco, broken parts from a plastic toy, a peace sign, a button that says Impeach Nixon, a baseball card of Carl Yazstremski, a program from his high school graduation in 1973, and a compass. She takes the compass, turns it in her hand, but the arrow points right at her no matter what she does. She shovels the stuff back into the box, takes the compass and places it in her pouch. She gets into bed with her pad of paper and writes, ⵏ'ⵏ ⵛⵛⵛⵛⵛⵛⵛ. (I'm scared.)

Then she lies down, holding the pouch to her chest as she tries to fall asleep, hoping her mother will be there soon.

Voices from downstairs awaken her like an electric shock, and at first, she doesn't know where she is. She can hear her mother and Nana downstairs—Mom crying and Nana talking to her. From the sound of the voices, she can tell something has changed.

After a long time, her mother comes up the stairs. Mona shuts her eyes and rolls over to pretend she's been sleeping, partly so she won't get in trouble for not going to bed, but also because she can't bear to have to hear the news yet. She can't bear to have her mother go through the telling. She doesn't want her mother to know that she was looking at the dead people in the book, that this might be her fault. Her mother opens the door quietly, slides off her shoes and drops her clothes on the floor. Then she lifts the covers and gets into bed with Mona. She sighs deeply and stifles a sob.

Shivering, she snuggles up to Mona and strokes her hair. "Mona, honey?"

Mona wants to roll over, to hug her, to cry with her, but she can't. Doing so will mean this horrible thing has really happened. Maybe, if they just fall asleep, they'll wake up in the morning and it all will be better. So Mona doesn't move, scarcely breathes. She pictures her father's heart and concentrates on making it as light as it can be, until it floats above them, lighter than the feather, lighter than air.

"Eunuchs" in *Pleiades: A Journal of New Writing, 32:2 Summer* 2012

"Skin Art" in *Blue Penny Quarterly*, September, 2012

"Cell Division" in *Karamu*, 2000

"Eskimo Pie," in *Karamu*, 2010

"LaTendra" in *China Grove #2*, 2014

"Alewives" in *Urban Spaghetti, vol. 2, issue 1*, 1999

"Rabbit's Foot" in *The Literary Review, vol.44, no. 3*, 2001

"Dust and Ice" in *The Newport Review Issue 3, Spring/Summer*, 2009

"Skating on the Vertical" in *Carve Magazine*, 2001

"Rocky Road" in *River Oak Review, no. 13, Fall* 2000

"Carbones Calientes" in *The Brucennial 2010 Miseducation, Literary Supplement*, 2010

"Mother's Helper" in *Ragnarok*, the e-journal of Valhalla Press, 2012

"Wedding Photo" in *Cease, Cows*," Nov. 2013 and in *Sunset Drinking the Black Ocean*, 2016

"Talisman" in *The Rockford Review. vol. XVII, no. 1, Winter*, 1998

"Weighing the Heart" in *Black Dirt, vol. 1, No. 1*, 1998

"Mother's Helper" won the Valhalla Press Literary Fiction Contest in 2012.

The collection, in a different version, was a finalist for the Flannery O'Connor Award in 2009.

"Alewives," "Rocky Road," "Dust and Ice," and "Talisman" were designated Runner-up for the Illinois Arts Council Fellowship in 2001.

"Weighing the Heart," "Rocky Road," and "Cell Division" were given Illinois Arts Council Awards for Prose (1999, 2001, 2001). "Rocky Road" won 1st prize in the River Oak-Hemingway Contest in 2000.

Acknowledgements

Many thanks to:

DONNA BISTER AND MARC ESTRIN at Fomite Press for their wisdom, professionalism, and continued support for my work

CAITLIN HAMILTON SUMMIE, a most excellent publicist, who balances solid advice with warmth

FRED SHAFER, master teacher, inspiring mentor, and the members of his short-story groups over the years as well as the offshoots of those groups: LAF, Writers' Bridge, and the Evanston Thursday Group. Great collaborative support, life blood for this writer

My Vermont College of Fine Arts mentors:
PHYLLIS BARBER, DIANE LEFER, ELLEN LESSER, PAMELA PAINTER, who helped me shape and bring these stories to life.

My VCFA cohorts: LIZ BUCHANAN, MARY BREAULT, JEN KIERNAN GAUDETTE, MARIE AND VINCE IGLESIAS-CARDINALE, DOREEN KEIFER KOPECKY, and GIGI THIBODEAU

DAN FRANK, principal at Francis W. Parker School, who gave me space in my teaching life to pursue my MFA

LORIN PRITIKIN, awesome friend and colleague, always quick to remind me, "That would make a good Jan Leary story."

MY STUDENTS at Francis W. Parker School and North-western University

THE EDITORS who originally published a number of these stories

THE ILLINOIS ARTS COUNCIL for their support

My parents, for filling my childhood with books and stories

JOHN LEARY, for his love, insightful reading of my drafts, and the beautiful cover painting

JAMES and WILLIAM LEARY, for being their wonderful selves and for tolerating my tendency to include anecdotes from their lives in my writing

Fomite

About Fomite

A fomite is a medium capable of transmitting infectious organisms from one individual to another.

"The activity of art is based on the capacity of people to be infected by the feelings of others." Tolstoy, What Is Art?

Writing a review on Amazon, Good Reads, Shelfari, Library Thing or other social media sites for readers will help the progress of independent publishing. To submit a review, go to the book page on any of the sites and follow the links for reviews. Books from independent presses rely on reader to reader communications.

For more information or to order any of our books, visit http://www.fomitepress.com/FOMITE/Our_Books.html

More Titles from Fomite...

Novels
Joshua Amses — *During This, Our Nadir*
Joshua Amses — *Raven or Crow*
Joshua Amses — *The Moment Before an Injury*
Jaysinh Birjepatel — *The Good Muslim of Jackson Heights*
Jaysinh Birjepatel — *Nothing Beside Remains*
David Brizer — *Victor Rand*
Paula Closson Buck — *Summer on the Cold War Planet*
Roger Coleman — *Skywreck Afternoons*
Marc Estrin — *Hyde*
Marc Estrin — *Kafka's Roach*
Marc Estrin — *Speckled Vanities*
Zdravka Evtimova — *In the Town of Joy and Peace*
Zdravka Evtimova — *Sinfonia Bulgarica*
Daniel Forbes — *Derail This Train Wreck*
Greg Guma — *Dons of Time*

Fomite

Richard Hawley — *The Three Lives of Jonathan Force*
Lamar Herrin — *Father Figure*
Ron Jacobs — *All the Sinners Saints*
Ron Jacobs — *Short Order Frame Up*
Ron Jacobs — *The Co-conspirator's Tale*
Scott Archer Jones — *A Rising Tide of People Swept Away*
Maggie Kast — *A Free Unsullied Land*
Darrell Kastin — *Shadowboxing with Bukowski*
Coleen Kearon — *Feminist on Fire*
Coleen Kearon — *#triggerwarning*
Jan Englis Leary — *Thicker Than Blood*
Diane Lefer — *Confessions of a Carnivore*
Rob Lenihan — *Born Speaking Lies*
Colin Mitchell — *Roadman*
Ilan Mochari — *Zinsky the Obscure*
Gregory Papadoyiannis — *The Baby Jazz*
Andy Potok — *My Father's Keeper*
Robert Rosenberg — *Isles of the Blind*
Ron Savage — *Voyeur in Tangier*
David Schein — *The Adoption*
Fred Skolnik — *Rafi's World*
Lynn Sloan — *Principles of Navigation*
L.E. Smith — *The Consequence of Gesture*
L.E. Smith — *Travers' Inferno*
Bob Sommer — *A Great Fullness*
Tom Walker — *A Day in the Life*
Susan V. Weiss — *My God, What Have We Done?*
Peter M. Wheelwright — *As It Is On Earth*
Suzie Wizowaty — *The Return of Jason Green*

Poetry
Antonello Borra — *Alfabestiario*
Antonello Borra — *AlphaBetaBestiaro*
James Connolly — *Picking Up the Bodies*
Greg Delanty — *Loosestrife*
Mason Drukman — *Drawing on Life*

Fomite

Stories

Fomite

Andrei Guriuanu — *Body of Work*
Derek Furr — *Semitones*
Derek Furr — *Suite for Three Voices*
Zeke Jarvis — *In A Family Way*
Marjorie Maddox — *What She Was Saying*
William Marquess — *Boom-shacka-lacka*
Gary Miller — *Museum of the Americas*
Jennifer Anne Moses — *Visiting Hours*
Peter Nash — *Parsimony*
Martin Ott — *Interrogations*
Jack Pulaski — *Love's Labours*
Charles Rafferty — *Saturday Night at Magellan's*
Kathryn Roberts — *Companion Plants*
Ron Savage — *What We Do For Love*
L.E. Smith — *Views Cost Extra*
Caitlin Hamilton Summie — *To Lay To Rest Our Ghosts*
Susan Thomas — *Among Angelic Orders*
Tom Walker — *Signed Confessions*
Silas Dent Zobal — *The Inconvenience of the Wings*

Plays
Stephen Goldberg — *Screwed and Other Plays*
Michele Markarian — *Unborn Children of Americ*

Odd Birds
Micheal Breiner — *the way none of this happened*
David Ross Gunn — *Cautionary Chronicles*
Gail Holst-Warhaft — *The Fall of Athens*
Roger Leboitz — *A Guide to the Western Slopes and the Outlying Area*
dug Nap— *Artsy Fartsy*
Delia Bell Robinson — A Shirtwaist Story
Peter Schumann — Planet Kasper, Volumes One and Two
Peter Schumann — Bread & Sentences
Peter Schumann — Faust 3
.Peter Schumann — We

57759338R00123

Made in the USA
Middletown, DE
18 December 2017